ELECTRICAL
STORMS

ELECTRICAL STORMS

A NOVEL
DAVID HOMEL

Random House
Toronto

Published in Canada in 1988 by Random House of Canada Limited.

Canadian Cataloguing in Publication Data

Homel, David
  Electrical Storms

Hardcover ISBN 0-394-22045-5
Quality Paperback ISBN 0-394-22081-1

I. Title.

PS8565.054E54   1988   C813'.54   C88-094478-1
PR9199.3.H65E54   1988

Jacket Design: Falcom Design & Communications Inc.
Jacket Illustration: Martin Dulac
Author Photograph: © 1988 Wenk

Printed and bound in Canada by T.H. Best Printing Company Limited

for the boys and girls of Kensington

ELECTRICAL STORMS

The War at Home

The 1960s begin.
     We are crouching on the cool tile floor in the hallway of Goodman Avenue School. Our behinds are on the floor, our hands are on the back of our heads, and our arms protect our faces. We are in fourth grade and we are waiting for the bombs to fall. We have been told that the bricks of Goodman Avenue School will shield us from the blast as long as we assume the correct position, like this. We listen for the drone of the planes overhead.

We used to listen for the locomotive roar of the tornado back when these were called storm drills. Mrs. Kovacs, our teacher, would remind us of the Good Friday twister that ran down Ninety-Fifth Street like a CTA bus and killed everybody who didn't go right away into the northwest corner of their basements for protection. But no one pretends any more. It's into the hallway, crouch down in the special position, wait for the bombs or the all clear.

The hall is perfectly quiet, like a church. I can smell the Right Guard that some of the older kids are beginning to use. Everybody is busy thinking about what would happen if the bombs really did fall this time, which of course could never happen. How we would all get wiped out like a firecracker in an anthill, not one at a time, where you can have your own death, like with a German machine-gun nest, rat-a-tat-tat, at the movies. I try to imagine all of us disappearing. Where would we go to? I picture the school not there but I don't know what to put in its place on the land where it stands. I have no trouble imagining the people gone—they could have moved away, or be on vacation. But the buildings, the city, the whole world . . .

Then all of a sudden Patti Schmidt throws up. A couple of the guys snigger, then they want to move away because it doesn't smell too good, but they can't because we're all too packed in. The throw-up is all red and runny, like hot dogs and tomato juice mixed up. Patti throws up every time there's a bomb drill. And no one can move or clean it up until the all clear, because what if this time it's really true? So the throw-up just sits there. The air in the hallway is starting to get pretty bad.

Then something incredible happens. Mr. Begvar, the Norwegian janitor, leads Patti away. They go down the hall and turn the corner, toward the bathroom. He's going to wash her up. He doesn't believe in the bomb drill, so why should we, especially since he's the oldest one in the school. We don't really believe in it anyway, who could? Mr. Begvar comes back with his mop; he has his work to do. A few of the older guys are edging off toward the end of the hall where the daylight comes in. Just in time, they sound the all clear.

That evening the headlines in our parents' papers read "Search or Sink." No homework has been assigned and we know why, though I don't ask my parents about it; I don't think anyone does. The older kids have started saying that there's sure to be a war over the ships we want to stop, the Russian ships that are just ninety miles from Miami Beach. We tell them that's impossible, that they're lying. It's a shocking lie, like saying that your parents aren't your real parents. The older kids tease us. They chant, "There's gonna be a war-war, there's gonna be a war-war!"

THERE'S ANOTHER WAR at home when my parents fight. My brother and I call it an electrical storm. My father is selling World Book now, going from one house to the next. At school we have to say what our fathers do. My father said to me, "Tell them your daddy works in an office." That's because he used to work in an office until he started selling World Book a couple of months ago. But I don't want to lie, and when it comes time I don't. Instead, I say, "My daddy sells World Book" because I like the name, the world in a book. Nobody laughs or makes fun of me. Maybe they don't know what selling World Book really means.

I found out why my father is selling World Book now, why he's not working at the museum any more. He used to make shows that people came to see. It was like working in an office, which is what all my friends' fathers do, or at least that's what they say they do, except that it was in a museum, with art.

It started with Gino Como coming over. He had been my father's friend since the Great Depression. It was a Saturday afternoon. I had come back from baseball. My mouth tasted like Dairy Queen and dirt. Gino and my father were drinking wine. My mother was shopping. "Have some more Dago red," Gino said to my father. They were red-faced on a Saturday afternoon, and they were remembering things. "Remember the time Old Joe Sheridan took off all his clothes and danced around on the tables?" "Crazy Wobblie!" They slapped each other on the back. It looked like fun.

My father said to me, "Gino was the greatest shovel leaner of all time. Shovel leaning with Gino was a two-man job, and you had to be sharp. He would lean, and you had to lean the other way so's he wouldn't fall over." This Great Depression they are always talking about doesn't sound so bad after all, with all this shovel leaning.

Then Gino said to me, "How come you got an Italian name, Vinnie? Vinnie's an Italian name, not a Jewish name."

I looked at him. What did I know about my name?

"I named him after Vincent van Gogh," my father said.

He was laughing. I didn't know this van Gogh. He wasn't a family member recently passed away.

Gino was waving his finger at my father. "That's not a kosher name!"

My father shrugged his shoulders. "Kosher? I gave it up for the revolution."

Gino and my father stopped to stare at each other, like when someone tells a joke and no one knows if it's funny yet. Then they tapped their cups together. They were drinking out of the coffee cups we got at Shell.

"To the revolution!"

Then Gino turned to me again. "Vinnie, boy, do you know your father here is a poet? That's right, a bona fide poet!"

My father started looking uncomfortable on the living-room couch. I couldn't tell if Gino was making fun of him or not.

"A real poet. He used to write about love in the factory. He was our shop-floor Shakespeare. Heaving breasts and bulging biceps. He wasn't no nature poet, oh, no! He didn't have tall trees: he had stacks of crates on the loading docks.''

For being a friend, Gino was sure making fun a lot.

"But now he's working in the art castle. They've got all those *fungoled* artists locked up in there. I can't believe it: an old *gumbad* has got the key.''

My father wasn't happy. I had heard of drunk before, when your head spins and you fall down. That's what Gino must have been.

"Come on, Lefty," my father said, "leave the kid alone."

"That reminds me: your father used to play in *Waiting for Lefty*.'' Gino raised his fist in the air. "Strike! Strike! Strike!''

He got up and poured himself some more wine, but he stayed standing, like he was on his way out.

"Your father's a poet," he insisted.

"My fires are banked," my father answered.

He sounded proud about it. But what are banked fires? Fires you put in the bank?

"I was a humanist," my father declared. Now it was his turn to start sounding drunk, saying all the things he was, and about his banked fires.

"I was a humanist. Even when my good-for-nothing brother Moe was making big money selling red pills to whorehouse bands and lying around the poolrooms, I clung to the higher values.''

Gino laughed. "Hey, cut it out with that talk about whorehouses. There's a kid around!''

Every kid hates being called a kid. Then there was the car pulling up outside with my mother in it, coming back from food shopping at the Jewel, and my father was pushing Gino out the back door with his Dago red bottles in his hands, and Gino was laughing, real silly. I wonder whatever happened to my father's poems.

I don't know exactly when it happened. Gino was over at the house more. He was telling my father things. "I don't know why you moved out of the old neighborhood. There a man isn't ashamed to have a nice cup of coffee at nine o'clock in the morning in a restaurant with the want ads.''

My father would answer him, "I didn't want my second born to have to sleep in a pulled-out dresser drawer like I did.''

That's me, the second born.

Then they would sit and look at their hands. Then my father would say something. "I didn't want to be the last white face on the block. What if some punk kid forgets I'm the Great White Liberal?"

Some of the things my father said to Gino he would say at the dinner table. "Russian socialist realist art in the heroic mode. The strength of my reputation based on the van Gogh show." Drunk sorts of things like that.

Then in the dark I heard my mother say, "You'll lose your job over those *meshuggeneh* Russians. You expect the First National Bank to be a patron of this?" The sound of turning over in bed. Then turning back. "You want a painting of the heroic girl defenders of Stalingrad? Why not my Uncle Sam? He's not a girl, he didn't wear a kerchief on his hair and a machine gun on his hip. He was sent to Siberia. Your Russians let him out long enough to defend Stalingrad and take Berlin, then they locked him up again. If death hadn't delivered him he would still be there."

There's only the wall between us. You can hear the light being turned out. Sometimes I think they forget I'm around, and that I'm only a child, and that I'm supposed to be having a childhood.

THIS IS HOW I learned to drink gin. I'm the only one in my class who does, I'm sure, and that makes me different, which is what my parents say I'm supposed to be. Not even my brother does, and he teaches me the capitals of the states after the lights are out. The capital of Delaware is Dover, the capital of Wyoming is Cheyenne, the capital of Illinois is Springfield.

It has to do with the fathers on the block who began to kill themselves. Mr. Tomson from across the street shot himself in the head. He had something wrong with him left over from Korea and he spent all day in a wheelchair. His wife ironed her clothes in front of him in a bikini and she used to send Danny out to Lil's candy shop to buy her Kotex. Danny was too embarrassed to, so I had to do it for him while he waited outside. That didn't bother me because I didn't know what Kotex were. Eric Wellman's father shot himself too. No one was surprised when they remembered that house with the blinds always drawn and Eric never going outside except for school. He played soldiers in the dark living room and had the biggest collection of men, tanks, trucks and ack-acks I'd ever seen, all in battle formation on the rug, where we weren't supposed to eat or drink anything. Except that all the men and all the equipment were German, and we used to call him Nasty Nazi before he moved away. Tina Clouds' father jumped in front of a passenger train, the California Zephyr. Bang! He got smeared all over the place. The police came walking up and down the tracks with black plastic bags picking up the pieces. People said that Mr. Dublin, who's his next-door neighbor, was pumping gas at his station, Frankie's and Eddie's, and he hears this thump and looks down and there's this hand lying right there at his feet. Except he doesn't know it's his next-door neighbor's hand. People said he had to take the rest of the day off.

During an electrical storm my father talks about how he understands Mr. Clouds, who we used to see standing on Brainard Avenue by the RR crossing. And I think of the other fathers on the block.

Except my father doesn't talk about killing himself; he says he wants to commit suicide, which are two words I don't know. After he talks like that he goes down into the basement, banging around in the air ducts that come out of the furnace, where it smells so sick of heating oil, bang, bang, bang, whatever it is down there that makes this house work the way it does, talking about a suicide and how he's going to go and commit it. From the way he says it, it must be something more shameful than selling World Book in this neighborhood where everybody is just barely hanging on and they'll kill you if you let go, where you have to say you work in an office.

Bang, bang, bang, in the pipes and ducts, then everything's quiet, he comes up later through the dark house and goes to bed. I wait up for him. Whatever a suicide is, he must have committed it.

Since World Book, my mother is working at Chicago Bridge and Iron in an office, like my father is supposed to be doing, on a temp job. I come back after school before she comes home and go down to the basement to look for the suicide. With a stepladder I can reach the top of the air ducts that make the banging noise. Sweep, sweep, sweep, my palm on the metal. Better wash before dinner. No suicide here, just dust. I move the ladder down a way. Then I come to it. It's hard and cool. I pick it up. It's the suicide. It's a bottle of gin. A bottle of gin hidden on top of an air duct in the basement of my house. Is this a suicide? What does the World Book say about it?

THERE ISN'T AN ELECTRICAL storm every night. Only two or three times a week, usually on weekends, after we've all been together. The other nights are calm. I can go down to the basement on my tiptoes, put the stepladder under the right spot and drink the gin. I have a metal tumbler that was part of a set my parents got a long time ago for opening a new bank account. I keep it hidden in the old toy chest and I told them I lost it outside. I fill the tumbler halfway up and I start to drink the gin. It's hard to keep down but I drink as much as I can stand, like medicine. What is supposed to happen now? I don't have time to think about it because I have to get back to my room in time. My parents go to bed after the ten o'clock news, but my father gets up later to walk around.

One thing the gin does, besides taste bad, is make you want to go to sleep. Maybe that's part of it being a suicide. My brother wakes up when I come back to our room. "What's that smell?" he asks. I don't want to tell him, I'm too ashamed. He doesn't wait for an answer. "It's Noxzema! Are you putting Noxzema on yourself?" "I'm putting it on my butt, do you want some?" I make him laugh and forget about the gin smell. The capital of California is Sacramento, the capital of Louisiana is Baton Rouge.

In our house, my father is the one who gets to stay up all night long and not sleep and walk around. He complains about how he has to do that, and how he has to sell World Book. My brother is getting pretty sick of it. He wants something to complain about too. You know they're going to go at it. My brother will start acting upset all the time so he can have something to complain about, but that doesn't really work, because the more he complains, the more my father complains and the more he walks around at night, so my brother's complaint gets lost in the shuffle. My father has his complaint; my brother has his too. I don't think there will be any room for me. That's all right—I don't like the way they go on complaining anyway. It's a little like when my father and my uncles and aunts get together, pretty soon they start shouting, "Excuse me for living!" and they're all trying to out-excuse each other for living. I'll be like my mother instead. She says, "If I carried on like the rest of you, there wouldn't be any family left." Maybe I'll just lie low a few more years, then get my due.

I HAVE A FRIEND named Keith who believes in God because his father is a minister in a church. "God is a crutch for weak people," my father likes to say. But the aunts and uncles are over for Passover anyway. It's the only holiday we really have in our house, though my father added Hanukkah at Christmas because once Keith came over and asked where the Christmas tree was. But Hanukkah isn't much. They light a candle and give me a penny or a nickel then blow out the candle before it burns down and save it for the next night.

But tonight the aunts and uncles are singing. I don't understand a word of it but I know they are singing about God. My father is singing too. Does he or doesn't he believe in God? At one point we all jump up from the table and rush to the door and throw it open to see if there is anyone who is hungry and wants to come in and have supper. There is no one. Not on this block. We close the door again. It's just as well because I wouldn't want any of my friends to see my aunts and uncles. They're short and fat and they talk funny and they're always sucking on hard candies.

They are Jews. With them, I think, it's more than not having a Christmas tree. They really are different. The way we're supposed to be.

During the dinner, I like the song about the plagues best. We're really happy that the Lord, blessed is he, did all these things to the Egyptians. My aunts and uncles are drinking the seventh glass of wine. I get to have some too. It tastes like pop. Every time there's a new plague we slam our palms down on the table. The glasses jump and the wine goes spilling on the tablecloth. Tonight is the only night nobody minds. Then comes the Angel of Death, a skeleton with wings flying through the air. He smites. That is the end of the song. We have won.

The aunts and uncles go home because they are tired. We pick up the table. There is the glass for Elijah the Prophet who can come knocking at the door any time during dinner, even at our door. You have to be ready for him with the glass of wine. My father picks it up. "I guess Elijah isn't going to come this year. What the hell!" My father drinks down the wine in one gulp. That seems to me to be the worst thing anyone has ever done in my presence. What about Elijah? If he comes and discovers his wine has been drunk, there will be a plague.

That night I have a bad dream. I wake up, my mother is there, my mouth tastes like metal, like a burnt transformer from an electric train. The house was being attacked by skeletons, like the kind they have at Halloween. My parents were there, I was there, my brother was there. But my parents couldn't defend us. They could only give warnings. "There's one over there! Quick!" The house was swarming with them. If they touched you you were dead. I swung one of the folding chairs left over from the aunts and uncles. The skeleton collapsed in a rattle of bones. I woke up.

MRS. KOVACS SAID we were going to have another drill. She made us promise not to make fun of Patti Schmidt if she threw up. "Patti is sensitive," Mrs. Kovacs told us. I've heard that word before. One of the singing aunts said, "I have a sensitive stomach." Sensitive means sick.

Patti Schmidt has fallout without the bomb.

My mother is trimming celery for the barley soup. Watching her trim celery is like reliving the Great Depression, from the first day to the last. My parents are always talking about the Great Depression, way-back-when, when you had to scrape and save, but here it is, in the kitchen of my own house. My mother cuts off only the very bottom of the stalk and leaves a lot of the brown part on, and she doesn't throw away the thin top branches with the wilted leaves that are all mushy-tasting. When I grow up, I don't want to be a fireman or a race-car driver or someone on the Ed Sullivan Show. I want to be able to throw away all the brown parts from a celery stalk.

Lately she's been cutting the celery even closer to the end because of Uncle Life. Uncle Life was her brother. He was living in one of those giant hotels that are all filled up with Indians and people with southern accents and old people. They called her to come and clean out his room because he had been sent to a hospital for people who couldn't take care of themselves any more. She was next of kin, which was a bad thing, judging from what happened next. I came along because no one knew any better. It turned out that Uncle Life collected things, which was part of why he couldn't take care of himself any more. He had bags and bags of playing cards and balls-and-jacks sets. He had stacks of matchbook covers, which is how I started my collection. There were big bags of some other stuff, too, but I didn't get to look inside. It smelled awful, like an old outhouse. Petey the Parakeet was dead in his cage. My mother got real upset, Uncle Life was her own flesh and blood, and look what happened to him. The smell was so bad tears were running down my cheeks and they took me out into the hallway. My mother kept scrubbing and cleaning up the room, even though no one she knew would ever live there again.

That was the first time I saw her so upset. The whole house stopped. There was no dinner. We went to Hasty Tasty for a hamburger, which wasn't as good as I had thought it would be. The next day she cried at the dinner table, into the barley soup. My brother said to her, "You can't cry." That made her cry even harder. It was a horrible thing that my brother said.

The little brown centers in the barley are like little eyes. A whole soup plate of eyes.

WITH ALL THE TALK about not sleeping at night, it makes sense that I would catch it too, like when someone in the house has a cold. I needed a complaint too, and this was a good one since it wouldn't bother people too much. Sometimes I stayed up to go downstairs when the house was quiet, sometimes I stayed up to read under the blanket with my penlight, but mostly I stayed up to be like my father.

I wanted to show him I could be like him. One night when he was walking around the house I got up and went into the living room where he was. I didn't know what I was going to do when I got there. There were no lights on. He was standing by the window with the drapes open and looking at the street. When I got into the room I was too afraid to speak or say Hi, Dad. I just stood there in the light that came in from the outside, so he would see me. He turned around and looked at me and then something horrible happened. He didn't see me at all and it wasn't because he wasn't wearing his glasses, he was. He just stared. He was in his own night. I turned around and stubbed my toe on the end table. Going to see him in the living room was the wrong thing to do.

At first I was proud of not sleeping, even if I couldn't walk around the house while my father did. One time when it was late, a weekend night with company over, I came out of my room. My father saw me. "What's the matter with you, can't you sleep?" he said. I thought about that. Maybe there was something the matter with me because I couldn't sleep.

OUTSIDE THE WALLS of our house, there is not going to be a war after all. The ships were stopped or searched; anyway, the Russians chickened out. There will be no war, but we had another war drill anyway. The drill bell rings in the school. "Enemy planes have been sighted! Quick, take shelter in the hallway!" Mrs. Kovacs, our teacher, calls. We all file out into the hall to put our heads between our knees. The floor is cool and gritty. I count how many little spots of color there are in each floor tile to pass the time. We don't feel protected by the bricks of Goodman Avenue School. We feel protected because the Russians won't fight and they let us search their boats. All of us except Patti Schmidt. She is sensitive. She throws up again. Mr. Begvar shuffles down the hall with his mop. There's something a lot less exciting about today's drill, since the war won't happen. Some of the older kids, the same ones who promised us a war the other day, try to slip out the door before the all clear. Mrs. Kovacs hisses in the quiet hallway, "Get back in here, you boys, the drill isn't over yet!" That doesn't work on them, they keep edging down the hallway. I know one of them has cigarettes and they want to go and smoke them.

Mrs. Kovacs tries to keep them in line. "If you go outside you'll all be killed. The bombs are falling!" Her voice gets real high at the end and everybody turns and looks at her. Boy, is she nervous, I wonder what about. She puts her hand over her mouth to catch her words but it's too late. Everybody is giggling. She can't punish all of us. Nobody can believe in the war.

At least not when we're all together like this. But I bet Patti Schmidt isn't the only one who wants to throw up when we're all crouching on the floor, smelling ourselves and waiting for the all clear. She's just the only one who does it.

AT HOME, I LIE low and wait for the electrical storms to pass over. After the ten o'clock news, and before midnight, I tiptoe down to the basement and commit the suicide. I still don't know what those words stand for, just like I thought there was a real hole in the field when I heard on the radio that Ernie Banks had slapped one into the hole on the left side. I don't mind drinking the stuff, I have to if I want to be grown-up, but in the morning when I sniff the tumbler in the toy chest, the smell makes me sick to my stomach.

IN SOCIAL STUDIES CLASS, the teacher tells us that America has won every war it ever fought in, and that we'll continue to win them all. But I know, and I know Patti Schmidt knows, there's one war you can never win: the war at home.

Kensington Krazies

2

The next time I saw Patti Schmidt was right at the end of the decade. The Goodman Avenue School veterans were having a Saturday afternoon cookout in the Cook County Forest Preserve, a kind of skid row for derelict trees. There was Patti, and Bobby Flynn and Blowy Bloedell, who had been smirking boys stealing off down to the end of the hall in search of fresh air, not believing in the war outside. And me, Vinnie Rabb, "Elephant Ears" according to Flynn, because I was willing to listen to Patti's predictable problems.

Chuck Alden was there too, that afternoon. He wasn't a Goodman Avenue School vet. Back in those days he lived in Benton Harbor, on the other side of Lake Michigan, where his father preached in an Anglican church and his mother gardened.

We called ourselves the Kensington Krazies. A second family. We devised it to replace our original families, so at war with themselves that they had forgotten all about us. That way we got to grow up faster.

The Jefferson Airplane had just come out with *Surrealistic Pillow* on a straight record label. The cookout was in celebration of that. If a straight record company was willing to put out our music, we figured, maybe the world really was going to change.

We were all standing around listening to "Somebody to Love" on a transistor radio one of us had gotten for being a good paperboy not so long ago. Patti was contemplating the steaks on the barbecue. All of a sudden she started screaming, "Dead meat! Dead meat!"

She whipped the steaks right off the hot grill and threw them on the ground. They were only blade steaks from the Jewel drowned in meat tenderizer, but what the hell. It was a waste.

Blowy picked them off the ground. They were all furred with dirt. I might have tried to brush them clean but Blowy didn't.

"These steaks are gone," he told us. Then he sidearmed them into Salt Creek.

Everybody was spooked; nobody knew what to do. Patti had done something crazy, but craziness was respected. That was our trademark. We were the Kensington Krazies. The Krazy family.

I led Patti over to the picnic table. We sat with our shoes on the bench, and I started the kind of systematic talk-down you use to calm people on bad acid trips. I had done it before with Blowy and Flynn. The first procedure: establish a common point of reference between the helper and the person freaking out. But the only memory that would come to me was the bomb drills in grammar school, and Patti throwing up, as predictable as the all clear at the end when the bomb hadn't fallen.

It wasn't a very good start to a talk designed to calm her troubled soul. I half expected another storm to burst from inside her thin, rattly body and wreck what was left of our cookout. But Patti smiled at the memory, dreamy and proud in a strange sort of way, and confided in me that she hadn't kept down a whole meal since the fourth grade. I took it all in, me, Vinnie Rabb, Yid priest, ad hoc member of the helping professions, pressed into service to hear this confession from a Kensington girl at war with her body.

Bobby Flynn came wheeling by. He looked at Patti's hand holding mine. The rewards of the helping professions.

"Go to it, Elephant Ears," he mock encouraged me. "Listen, everybody wants to leave. The atmosphere is shot. And you can't have a cookout without meat."

I steered Patti toward Blowy's silver Chevy station wagon, which he called Angel. I'd put the gas money in this time, so I got to sit behind the wheel. Patti was next to me, holding my hand. Flynn was by the window. Blowy was in back, not worried about someone else driving Angel. Charles Alden sat straight next to him. And behind us all, Angel's rear end swaying like a fish.

It was a quiet ride back to where Kensington's houses were. We were all waiting for Patti Schmidt to get out. It was like being in a hospital suite on wheels.

I stopped Angel in front of Patti's place. She squinted through the windshield at her two-flat.

"I better go now." Her voice was tiny. "I fix dinner for my mother. She's sick."

Then she turned and kissed me. A bad smell came from her mouth, as if deep down she was eating herself up from inside. In front, her hair was thin like an old lady's.

Flynn got out to let her out. He slammed the door loud when he got back in, as if he were waking us from hypnosis.

"I paid for those steaks," Blowy complained. "I want my money back."

"She was just expressing herself," Charles Alden told him.

Bobby Flynn looked at Alden as if he had just landed from Mars. "What're you going to do about her, Elephant Ears?"

"Not let her anywhere near my fridge," I answered Flynn. "And remember, before you call me Elephant Ears again, you're in the death seat."

I turned the car toward Kensington's black side of town.

"I vote we get us some beer. It's an uncool high, but I bet it'll fix the vibrations."

We drove down into Kensington's little black ghetto. It was at the bottom of a steep hill, where Lake Michigan used to come up to. When Kensington got started after the Chicago Fire, there were marshes at the bottom of the hill that no one could drain, and that's where they put the blacks. After the Fire, you weren't allowed to build wood houses any more in Chicago. Kensington was invented for people who still wanted to build a wood house.

I knocked on Mrs. Hooper's door. She had a game show on. She yelled for me to come in.

"Can you do us a favor, Mrs. Hooper?"

"Of course, of course I can." She was the fattest woman I had ever seen. "If it weren't for you white boys needing your beer, I wouldn't get out of the house at all."

"Here's the money. Get us whatever you can, and save something for yourself."

"Of course I will." She laughed. "I don't drink beer myself but my Albert likes a cool one when he comes home from work. Now you just sit right down here and wait and I'll be right back."

She waddled out the door to the package store. On her coffee table was a box of chocolates and some *Ebony* magazines. *Ebony* was just like *Life* except all the people had tan faces. If you came from another planet and saw *Ebony*, you would think there wasn't any such thing as white people, and if there were, that they didn't live any different from blacks.

I changed the channel to Divorce Court and was lost in it when Mrs. Hooper came back. She had two six-packs of Drewry's for us. "I don't know what that liquor-store man is going to think of me."

She handed me the bag and sat down in her chair. She saw Divorce Court was on TV. "You're watching that program? You must like other people's troubles."

I changed it back to the game show for her.

"Now, give me what I want." She smiled.

I went and kneeled down in front of her. She took my head and buried it between her breasts. I closed my eyes and let it happen. She smelled like loaves of bread. "My Albert used to let me do this when we were courting." Her voice was far away. "Not any more. Men!"

Then she turned me loose. "Take your beer. And if you get caught don't tell Mr. Man where you get that stuff!"

She laughed. "You're old enough to be a soldier, but you're not old enough to have you a beer!"

THE NATURAL HISTORY of the decline of Kensington: a good place to live for wooden-house builders. The natural history of the decline of the old suburbs, peopled by the Bohunks of Bohunk heaven. On the Ogden Avenue strip they opened their New Bohemia taps and their Old Praha lounges and over a shot and a beer they could reflect on their long slow climb from the floor of the steel mill to the foreman's job. They were there to stay. Only Kensington, where they had bought their homes, wasn't. Something invisible and insidious that sounded like science fiction was occurring: the erosion of the tax base. On Kensington's main drag, the storefronts were emptying. The big five-and-dimes like Montgomery Wards and Kresge's, with their bright purple and orange fountain drinks, were heading for the shopping centers where the parking was easy. The small assembly plants that gave us all work in the summer found that in exurbia, the taxes on their parking lots were lower. Besides, the closer they were to the cornfields, the less the danger of unions. Half the storefronts in downtown Kensington were empty. The Southwest Side Community Center for Mental Health rented most of the old Kresge's.

My parents bought their 50 by 150 lot and moved into Kensington when little unplanned Vinnie came along. A hole in a Sheik was to blame, no doubt. It was an odd choice of neighborhood; once my father had treasured living among the earnest, bearded intellectuals of Hyde Park. Then suddenly we were packed off to Kensington to live among the wooden-house builders, descendants of people who had vaulted up to Orthodox heaven more quickly for having persecuted our grandfathers. No more coffeehouses or stands selling the *Daily Forward*. This is the fruit of banked fires. We became suburbanites just as the suburbs were beginning to fall apart.

SOMETHING INSIDIOUS WAS HAPPENING to Patti Schmidt too. I listened to all I could stand; listening changed nothing. Patti's skin was flaking. Her hair was thin. She couldn't talk about anything but what she was going to fix for her sick mother's dinner. I wanted to tell her to go see a shrink, but the Kensington Krazies were against shrinks. Where would we be if we weren't crazy? Where would Patti be without her problem?

Meanwhile, we had turned into a double-income family. My father shuffling papers at the Veterans' Admin with a bunch of black ladies, and my mother flipping file cards at a factory that made water pumps in Kensington's waning industrial park. That left the house empty in the afternoon for Patti and me. We were having the same talk we always had. Vinnie Rabb, layman shrink, eager to rummage around under Patti's blue Sears work shirt before the five o'clock whistle blew and the workers came home.

I put on the old Verve recording of "Music for Zen Meditation." Rumor had it that it calmed the spirit. Then Patti surprised me.

"You can take off my clothes if you want to," she told me. "I want to go all the way."

Her body was like a boy's. Two hard knobs on her chest for

breasts. Her hips were flat and fleshless, conjuring up enormous loneliness in me. The Zen music twanged and whistled in the background.

Patti peeled back the bedspread and lay down naked with her palms flat on the sheets, as if she were on an operating table. I had a flash of the Camps. A survivor in my bed, in Kensington. I was undone.

"I don't think we should do it." I grasped for the first excuse. "It's only safe when you're on your period."

Patti jumped out of bed and grabbed her shirt and jeans.

"You don't want to do it!" Her voice was a shriek. She started toward the door in just her pants.

"For God's sake put on your shirt!"

"I'm going to tell my mother we did it! I'm going to tell her you put your hand on my breast!"

You don't have any such part, I felt like telling her. I kept quiet instead. I was grateful when she was out of the house with her shirt and pants on and her shoes on the right feet.

THE NEXT DAY PATTI was in the Edge, the local loony bin. This mother of hers, whom I had never seen and who was always so sick, must have risen up from her bed to commit her. Patti had turned violent that night. With all seventy pounds, she had swung a Teflon frying pan and clanged her mother on the back of the head.

The male side of the Kensington Krazies met at the Spot to discuss it. Me and Charles Alden, Flynn and Blowy. Blowy ordered lemon-cream pie and coffee.

"Patti's in the Edge," I said. "I don't know what to do about it."

"Nothing," Flynn said. "There's nothing you can do about it."

"Don't take it personally," Alden said. "My girlfriend was in there too."

"Lo went too? What did she do?"

"Cut her wrists. In the rec room."

"Jesus Christ!"

"It wasn't for real," Alden said, "she cut crosswise, not lengthwise." He explained it all for us. "There's no way you can die if you cut at right angles to the vein. It's just an attention-getting device."

"You sound like some kind of shrink at the Edge," Flynn said.

"That's exactly where Lo went."

"What did they do with her there?" I asked.

"Nothing. What else would they do? Lo said the shrinks just talk to you, they make you talk about your problem. Once you admit you have a problem, they're happy. And of course the better you can talk the more they like you. They let up on you, they tell you to rest. They give you tranks to help you on your way. Then they turn you loose."

"You start all over again."

"That's right," Alden said.

We all listened to the downer hanging in the air, put there by Alden's explanations about the vein.

Flynn watched Blowy finish his lemon pie. When Blowy finished, he talked.

"Those girl problems are fucked anyway. Blowy here just got his draft notice. *That's* a real problem."

"I got to take a physical and I don't know what to do," Blowy said.

"What do you mean? You resist—that's what you do."

"I don't think I know how to resist."

"See a draft counselor. Shit, Blowy," I said, "we can't be losing any Kensington Krazies to Vietnam. There aren't enough of us."

Blowy shrugged. It didn't look too good for him. He didn't have enough fight. He was too much of a hippie.

We left the coffee shop. A block away on Calendar Avenue the new pedestrian mall was being inaugurated. Kensington was attacking the shopping centers on their own ground. You would not have to pay for parking any more. There were little fountains and plastic buckets of pansies just like at Oakbrook or any of the big malls. The street was blocked and the city had put potted evergreens where the cars used to park. There was even a roof over the sidewalk that made it look like a carport. A few pensioners stood around and watched the mayor cut the ribbon. A photographer from *Suburban Life* took pictures.

We got the usual hostile looks for being who we were. As if it was all our fault that the tax base had eroded away and there were weeds growing up through the cracks in the streets.

I SAW PATTI SCHMIDT ten days later. She was out of the Edge. This was one Edge you always came back from. Patti was absolutely triumphant.

"I got a transactionalist," she said, and I understood she was talking about her shrink. "He couldn't understand why a bright attractive young woman like myself didn't want to live a normal life. So I told him I did." Her eyes were shining. She was delighted: she had just worked her control trip over a shrink fresh out of med school. It was better than fixing dinner for her sick mother. "But I didn't want to make it look too simple. I told him I had a hard time accepting myself. I made a few confessions. I promised I wouldn't hit my mother over the head with a frying pan any more."

"That was probably the only healthy thing you ever did."

That imprudent line must have ended it. A few warm nights later we were out in Shawmut Park, where I had thrown my best sidearm curves a few years before for the Dick Chess Dodge little-league team. We had stockpiled Mrs. Hooper's beer and now we were sitting back watching the slow freights of the Indiana Harbor Belt switching and changing cars, listening to the click-click of the traffic over the expansion joints on the Ogden Avenue bridge. The cops came by for their Saturday evening sweep. We laid low and let their spotlights go overhead, but Alden and Patti Schmidt must not have heard the cop cars crunching over the gravel parking lot. At the worst possible time, Alden stood up and we saw his penis sticking up like a mushroom, wilting at the speed of light. The cops stopped and called through their bullhorn, "All right, you two, get dressed and get a move on."

And Alden did. He came tearing out of the bushes, pulling on his pants, clenching his fist in the spotlight.

"Deny the flesh! Mortify the flesh!"

He was crazed. The cops laughed nervously into their bullhorn. "Next time keep your behind down, son!"

But Alden was into it. Something had snapped in his head. "Come on, everybody!" He raised us out of the thicket where we were laying down with our six-packs of Drewry's. "Come on, mortify the flesh! Deny the flesh! Mortify the flesh!"

The cops wheeled away. Alden charged out of the darkness of the park toward downtown Kensington.

"Deny the flesh! Mortify the flesh!"

We all got into it. We thought we were mocking prudish, old, cautious Kensington. We ran after him, hollering his slogan. I caught up with him in a dozen strides; I had my cross-country legs and Alden was no athlete. But when I got a good look at him I eased my stride and fell back. His shirt was open and flapping; he had a wild look on his face like some kind of martyr about to be torn apart by wolves for the glory and example of Jesus Christ. He wasn't having any fun at all.

He stopped and turned on me. He was out of breath.

"Mortify the flesh! Don't you want to mortify the flesh?"

I looked at his flat bony chest shining in the streetlights under his open shirt.

"No, I don't," I told him. "I don't want to mortify the flesh."

I looked around for help. I didn't know what to do with Alden. Fifty yards behind us, Blowy and Flynn were standing, watching, with their hands on their hips. They could not hear what we were saying. Farther back Janie James had her hands cupped around her mouth and was hooting "Deny the flesh!" in her derisive way. Patti Schmidt was struggling to catch up with us. She did not have much strength in her body.

I put my arm around Alden's shoulder.

"Forget mortifying your flesh with Patti. I'll walk you home."

He dropped Patti Schmidt that quickly. We left the Krazies on the dark Shawmut Park diamond and walked up the steep Lake Michigan hill past the YMCA where the transients lived. We came up to the Burlington tracks, where the late-night commuter conductors were throwing bundles of tomorrow morning's papers off at the Kensington stop. At that moment, Kensington seemed to have a modest kind of harmony. The men going in and out of the News Agency for cigars, the lights flicking off in the display window of Koshgarian's rug company, the one or two commuters choosing the Friendly Tap, where the Miller sign glowed, over the taxis lined up at the curb. There was a place for everyone except us.

We turned onto Waiola Avenue. "Waiola" must have meant "underground spring that eats at your foundation" in the local Indian language. A river ran under the street, making the houses settle at odd tilting angles. They were giant structures, some from Civil War days, impossible buildings to heat, places where a child could wander off and get lost and not be found until he had almost starved. The houses had been divided unthinkingly into apartments over the years. Here was where the Reverend Alden had settled with his wife and one son.

We walked into the vestibule. A half-dozen mailboxes, none with names.

"An odd place for a priest to live."

"A minister; we're Anglicans," Alden corrected me. "You mean you haven't heard the news? Of course not—as a Hebrew you're not in the circuit."

We pushed our way through the second set of doors as Alden prepared his key.

"It seems we've fallen among thieves," Alden said, with the pride of scandal in his voice. "My father lost his church. He got caught with the wife of one of the churchmen. And believe it or not, it happened right in the church building."

He held the door to his apartment open. "I guess he got his places of worship mixed up."

I didn't know whether to joke along or commiserate. I suppose that was the way Alden engineered it.

"Where is he now?" I asked.

"My parents are talking to each other in supervised conditions. Marriage counselor."

"And so you've taken to mortifying the flesh now."

Alden didn't care for the comment. We went through the dark front room into the kitchen, where a light on the electric range glowed. There was a photo of the reverend and the missus on the wall. It must have been taken in the Benton Harbor period, before they moved to town. In it, his wife was a wispy country woman holding onto a pair of gardening gloves, her colorless eyes far away, as if she were staring across a field at nothing in particular. The reverend had a wrestler's body and a baby face that ended abruptly in a stringy-meat tangle of skin around his Adam's apple.

I couldn't blame the reverend for stepping out, even if his method was too obvious for my taste. Even a still photo told how his wife and son had ganged up to turn the man out. His gnarled hands and the protruding tendons in his neck made him look too massive for this house.

We sat down around the Formica table. The fluorescent tube buzzed on the range.

"You rescued me from Patti," he said, turning to me, "now what do you want to say?"

"I didn't want you to help the cops help you mortify your flesh. They did you a favor by turning away when you blew out of those bushes."

Alden shrugged his shoulders. He stood up and opened the cupboards. I saw that his family shopped where mine did. Saltines, cheerful orange macaroni and cheese, canned salmon that could be made into fish burgers, fried in bread crumbs and eaten with ketchup.

"I want to eat something," Alden said after a minute.

He got out a box of breakfast-cereal cubes and shook some onto the table. There are moments when the commonest of objects looks unreal, and this was one of them. Alden tried to ingest one of the squares of wheat filaments, but it wouldn't go down. He stood up, strode across the room and shook his fist at the Jesus portrait over the table.

Behold my visible heart, the Jesus portrait was saying.

"Deny the flesh! Mortify the flesh!" Alden howled at it.

Then he crashed back on his chair with a laugh of nervous exhaustion.

HAVING THE JEFFERSON AIRPLANE record for a straight record company turned out to be a mixed blessing. Free love and long hair were in *Time* magazine. Hippies started to be a new fashion.

Actually, we were pretty lousy hippies. I wore a black T-shirt, blue jeans and steel-toed engineer's boots at all times, except during cross-country practice. Charles Alden was like Cotton Mather with a nylon-stringed guitar. Blowy was the closest thing we had to a hippie: he said the word "vibrations" and meant it seriously, and all he wanted was to go on working for the landscaping firm, with his portable radio on the dash of the Step-Van tuned into one of the new FM stations, happy to be unrolling sod on well-turned dirt with a bunch of Mexicans. Flynn had been Blowy's friend since grade school; he just naturally came along. Our girlfriends' rebellion was sheer maladjustment with the way they were supposed to be in society, with the bodies that had been doled out to them. And they took it out on their bodies. Patti was starving herself to death, I was beginning to understand. Lo, who was a beautifully made Italian girl, cut at her wrists. Janie James made herself look as aggressive as possible; she peroxided her hair orange and wore skirts to the top of her thighs to show Kensington just how needle-thin her legs were. The girls had it worse than we did. We were expected to be a little delinquent. They didn't have the same release.

The only thing hippie about us was the absence of jealousy. When Alden and Patti Schmidt popped out of the bushes, it didn't bother me. They were two bodies made for each other. Unfortunately, that appearance of freedom attracted the same kind of people who had wanted to beat us up a few months earlier. They had heard about us on TV, they rubbed their hands together, they were ready for a summer of love. I had no use for any of them. Most of them were trash who had grown up in trailer parks watching soap operas in an odor of neglect while their mothers drank 7 and 7s all day, for whom Wonder Bread and Velveeta cheese food was a square meal, and whose only idea of where they came from was being able to tell each other to go sodomize themselves in Polish or Italian. I looked around at some of the hangers-on and saw that the gentle Kensington Krazies were in danger of being out-crazied by the straights.

THAT'S HOW TOM MAYO came to us. He rolled into the Spot coffee shop, which we called the Blot, on the backs of his heels like he had all winter, punching one hand into another. Only this time he did not slam his fist on the table and make the coffee cups jump out of their saucers like he usually did. He had seen the psychedelic record jackets and heard about the braless girls.

Janie James and Patti were there. And Lo, moping, with her long black hair sweeping the ashtray. And me and Alden.

We were at a booth for six. Mayo went to sit down next to Alden, but Jane stretched her legs out and put them on the seat where he wanted to be. He couldn't push her feet away. She was a girl.

He held up two fingers for the peace sign.

"Peace, man."

Alden looked at him as if he were some kind of trained bear who had learned to recite the Lord's Prayer. He flashed Mayo a peace sign back. Then he stuck his tongue through the V and wiggled it.

"A piece, man."

Then he turned his peace sign into a pointed gun.

"A piece, man."

I didn't get the game Alden was playing, but I did know he was way out of his league with that kind of talk. Mayo sensed it too. He pushed him a little bit further.

"Hey, man, got any dex or bennies?"

Alden cocked his head. "Ducks or bunnies?"

Mayo made like he didn't hear. "I want to get high, man."

He wanted the body drug.

"High on ducks and bunnies?"

Mayo was nervous. He had never talked to people like us before. He shifted his weight, he pounded his hands together. Our very own soft, downy Charles Alden reckoned his chances of plugging into Tom Mayo's power.

He strung Mayo along. It was like a flirtation thing. "You'll have your ducks and bunnies," he told him, "but first I have to see if you're cool. Go to Walgreen's and shoplift us half a dozen bottles of Robitussin Extra Strength DM. Make sure it's got the miracle drug dextramophorathan in it."

He spelled out "dextramophorathan" letter by letter. "And meet us tomorrow night in Shawmut Park at nine."

Mayo had a set of orders; he could relate to that. He went away satisfied. There would be drugs and he would not even have to wear flowers in his hair to score them.

"What do you want out of him?" I asked Alden. "Where's your memory? Don't you remember he punched you in the stomach last year because you were carrying a guitar?"

"He hit you so hard you threw up," Patti reminded him.

"Haven't you ever read Jean Genêt?" Alden asked me.

"No. Should I?"

"Yes. He says the hoodlum is a kind of poet. He's a saint. He's really deeply looking for affection. He's against society the way it is—and so are we. Can't you see that? Anyway, don't you think people can change?"

That was the hippie thing: change. If it's a change it must be good. *My mind is going through so many changes . . .*

"He's gonna change your face around," I told Alden.

NINE O'CLOCK AT SHAWMUT PARK. Us Krazies liked it because it had that industrial romance, the train yards, the long Ogden Avenue bridge. It made us feel square in the belly of the beast. The first true warm night, and all the troops were out to see what would give between Mayo and Alden.

Me and Blowy smoked a little grass out by second base on one of the diamonds. I had my glove and a hardball; Blowy had his. I never went anywhere without my mitt. Once a pitcher, always a pitcher.

"Come on, Blowy, get behind the plate. I'll pitch you one."

Blowy dusted off the invisible plate. Sandy Koufax might have had a better record, he might have refused to pitch on Yom Kippur, but I liked Drysdale's big sweeping motion better. I pitched Blowy a few big sidearm curves and fastballs that broke down and away from the right-handed hitter. The left-handed hitters were jammed. They hit infield pop-ups off their wrists. I got out of the inning.

"Okay, Blowy, get out your pancake, it's knuckleball time."

I had not yet perfected my knuckler. It bounced in on Blowy and skittered away toward where Alden was standing tearing at his fingernails.

He picked the ball up. He wanted to throw it to me. He took a few skip steps in my direction, cocked his arm way back behind his shoulder and released the ball. It rolled into my mitt.

"Hey, Alden," Blowy called, "my mama's got a better arm than you do."

Then Mayo showed. He brought a friend. We met them on

the foul side of third, going toward the grassy embankment up to the railroad right-of-way where everyone else was. Weaver was the friend's name, or Willer, with his pronunciation you could hardly tell. He could have been twenty-one, he could have been forty, with vacant suspicious eyes and a border-state drawl that said "hick" to anyone from the city.

Mayo looked around. "Do the cops come down here?"

Blowy nudged Alden with his elbow. "Hardly at all. And as long as you keep your ass down the motherfuckers don't see you."

"I live with my mother," Weaver informed us, "and nobody has the right to say that word, not as long as I'm around."

That put a damper on the conversation for a while. Weaver folded his arms and sank into silence. We drifted over to the embankment with Alden leading the way. I popped the ball into the pocket of my mitt.

Mayo sat down between Janie James and Patti Schmidt. He had six bottles of Robitussin in his windbreaker. He handed them over to Alden.

"That's the stuff!" Alden was real proud of his baby. "Here's one for you. You've got to get through the sugar and the excipient. Once you do there's codeine inside."

"It makes your right eye go left and your left eye go right," I told Mayo. "You won't see God but it takes your mind off your troubles."

We sprawled in grass that was already clammy with dew. Blowy lit another joint. I passed. Mayo was in on it. He must have thought he'd died and gone to hippie heaven. He drank his Robitussin like it was a can of beer.

Then the inevitable happened. Mayo clutched at his gut and crawled away crab style to retch up every drop of the stuff.

"Uncool," I said to Alden.

He was smiling. "Exactly."

A minute later Mayo came back from being sick, fully recovered and looking for some way to act high. "I'm stoned, man, I'm fucking stoned," he insisted.

It could hardly have been the case, since he'd thrown up every drop of Robitussin in the coach's box out by third base. Six foot two of pathological, trashy meat trying to be hip and high. Then he found a way. He fastened onto Janie James in her black turtleneck and immensely short leather skirt. Mayo must have had enough primitive intelligence to sense her uncaring attitude toward her body. He crawled over to her and put his head on her lap. She patted his hair, half maternal, half in distaste. Then he rose up on his knees and fell on top of her and they rolled a little down the embankment. He tried to kiss her, she wouldn't have it, then he pushed her skirt up and fumbled around between her legs. When he found his way in they started going to it. A couple of minutes later it was over. We hadn't done anything. He hadn't raped her. He'd just overpowered her and she hadn't fought back. It never occurred to us that we could have made a decision. What could we have said? "Excuse me, would you please stop fucking Janie James, she belongs to us''?

I guess we just weren't equipped to handle it.

TWO DAYS LATER, on the Monday, we were at the Spot. Janie James wasn't there. She had not been a Kensington Krazy since the night in Shawmut Park.

"That's it for Mayo," I told Charles Alden. "He's a destructive force. We don't need that."

"How come? Because he ripped a piece off one of our girls? Maybe she wanted it. Why don't you ask her?"

"What kind of language is that? You trying to talk like Mayo or what?"

I figured Patti or Lo would jump in too. They didn't. They were too contemptful and scared of their bodies to care what anyone else did with them.

"Don't forget," Alden pushed on, "Janie James never did anything. She never pushed him away. She never did anything to make me think she didn't want to. You're the only one telling me she didn't want to fuck Mayo."

That was pure Alden: he could out-talk any of us. Take what you knew was right instinctively and make you wonder, *Maybe I'm wrong...* Maybe Janie James wanted to ball Mayo. Add that to his ostentatious sensitivity, him showing us the pages of his journal all written in carefully with poetry and decorated with candle wax—the combination was hard to beat. He was a pure preacher's son, I was starting to see. And while his father was busy betraying Jesus Christ in word and deed, within the very walls where His spirit dwelled, Chuck was making up for the fault. Not by becoming more religious; by passing judgment right and left, on everything around him, including himself.

Tom Mayo saved us from further conversation. He came in with Weaver, and Alden saw him first. Alden began quacking and he put his hands to the side of his head like ears and rotated them.

Mayo did not get the joke. Alden let out a high-pitched laugh.

"Ducks and bunnies, Mayo, don't you get it?"

We all laughed along with Alden. Mayo must have felt like the class idiot. He must have had that feeling a lot, which didn't mean he liked it any more. Weaver was at his side, looking stunned and sallow and dangerous, even compared to Mayo. I made a mental note not to say "motherfucker."

"You promised me you'd get me some stuff." Mayo's voice was whining and plaintive in a strange sort of way.

"I didn't promise you," Alden corrected him in his best Sunday-school voice. "I said I'd try."

"You better do what you said! I'm not going to take any shit off hippies!"

"Is that so?" Alden licked his lips. "I'll see what I can do. I might be able to get you something by this weekend or next. In the meantime, if you want to get high, try some dextramophorathan. It worked for you last time."

I was amazed. Alden was acting like a Catholic schoolgirl showing a little tit. Working Mayo both ways, cutting him down then telling him he was the only one who could give him what he wanted.

Weaver was the only other one who knew what was going on.

"You're nothing," I heard him say to Mayo as they walked out of the Blot.

After they left, Blowy got real interested in Alden. "I didn't know you could get any amphetamines. If I went to my medical really speeding—"

"I can't get any."

"You can't?" Vietnam moved a little closer.

"If you can't," I asked Alden, "how come you told him you could?"

"Oh, I don't know. Just to see what he'd do."

"What are you going to do when he wants to collect?" Blowy asked.

"I'm not entirely sure."

Alden laughed, sharp and nervous. End of conversation. We were letting the incident go by, the way we had with Janie James. We weren't such great communicators, despite all our talk about communication. We had grown up in silent, angry houses. We had learned to brood along with those who raised us, then erupt into self-destructive violence. When it happened we would claim we didn't understand our own motives.

I DON'T KNOW what came over me, but the nights I hung around the house, when there was nothing happening with the Krazies, I started asking my father about the world of the singing aunts and uncles. Where they had come from, what their real names had been, what they did when they came here. Whether there was sin in their religion, and mortification and denial, the way there was in what Alden believed in.

My father wanted to know what was wrong with me.

"Are you going Jewish on me?" he asked.

"Not Jew-ish; Jew," I told him.

That made him angry, as I knew it would.

"You want to see Jews?" he challenged me. "I'll show you Jews!"

Fifteen minutes later we were driving on the Stevenson Expressway, a road that ran on stilts above the black ghettos. In one of those ghettos, he told me, my Uncle Moe had had his misfortune.

My mother turned to me in the backseat. "You never met your Uncle Moe."

"That's because he's a no-good scum," my father spelled it out for me.

The two of them burst into argument.

"I can call him that if I want to—he's *my* brother!" The car swung left and right as my father banged out his points on the Dodge's steering wheel. People gliding by in their faster cars turned to look at us waving our arms around inside ours. My parents started arguing in Yiddish. I don't understand Yiddish, but I knew what they were saying, probably because I knew what they were going to say before they said it. There were only so many things you could say in a family argument, no matter what language you said them in.

It turned out that Moe, who was long past retirement age, held onto a job working for a company that sold fridges and washing machines to black people who couldn't afford them and who didn't understand how credit worked. His role was to go to their houses and hand them repossession notices. To my father's pleasure, Moe had been shot in the stomach. To double his pleasure Moe had not died, so now he could show him to me, as an example of the kind of Jew, I suppose, that had made him stop wanting to be a Jew.

Uncle Moe's hospital was in Albany Park. It was Saturday. The hospital had a Sabbath elevator, which stopped at every floor automatically, so that no one had to push a button.

Moe was on the fifth floor. It was a long ride up with the doors opening and closing at every level.

"Hypocrites," my father said. "Where in the Good Book does it say anything about elevator buttons?"

My mother shushed him. She need not have. There was no one else in the elevator to hear his satire. It was more like a habit.

We gathered around Moe's bed in the usual formation.

"Here—a Jew," my father said as if we were medical students at the bedside of some freak of nature. "A *chazar* bill collector who got what he deserved." He turned to Moe. "You give all Jews a bad name. You're against everything I worked for all my life!"

Moe was not in a position to fight back. He was attached to an IV bottle and his skin was an off color, the color of dirty sheets.

"Yeah?" he said weakly, "and what have you done for the revolution lately?" He waved his hands in the air. "You were always an excitable young man. Well, I'm glad you care about what's happened to me, because I don't."

It's hard to argue with a man who claims to be a corpse, and even looks the part. My father sensed it.

"You have any questions for him?" he asked me. "Say, about sin and forgiveness, or the great tradition of learning among the Jews?"

I didn't have any questions.

My father insulted Moe a little more, halfheartedly, it's true, then we filed out of his hospital room for the long trip down in the Sabbath elevator. On the way home along the Stevenson, my father was triumphant. I was beginning to understand how we ended up in Kensington, the only Jews on the block.

I CALLED ON ALDEN a few days later. I didn't want to let him carry through his romance with Mayo without protesting a little. I knew Bobby Flynn and Blowy were not going to intercede. They had no use for Alden, with his sensitivity that could flip-flop on you and turn nasty and moralistic and self-hating.

Alden welcomed me into his apartment. It was a house of closed doors today. Every room had a door between it and the next room, and every door was closed.

"Can we talk?" I asked him.

"The reverend's gone."

"For good?"

"He got voted out of the church last night. He's off investigating new careers."

We had plastic slipcovers on our sofa. At Alden's place there were colorful crocheted coverlets made by the reverend's wife. She was good with her hands. She had an eye for design. Her boy Charles must have inherited his artistic side from her.

"I told Lo I was breaking up with her," he told me as we opened doors on the way to the back of the apartment.

"I figured that the other night in the park. You know, when you and Patti were mortifying the flesh together."

I would have kept Lo. She was much prettier than what any of us deserved, black hair and eyes and that nut-colored skin. The idea of her hurting that skin with her father's Wilkinson blade, even if it was only at right angles to the vein, made me want to cry for mercy.

"It wasn't real with Lo," Alden tried to explain. "She didn't understand my music. She isn't a musician herself."

"She threw her violin at the wall and broke it because she couldn't reach the notes she wanted to," I reminded him. "That should count for something with you."

He shrugged it off. "It was really only masturbation against the walls of the vagina."

Wall me up, I thought, like the throbbing heart in the Poe story. But I hazarded no such improper images in front of Charles Alden. He preferred the washboard-ribbed Schmidt.

"I don't see how you do it. I mean, with Patti."

Alden released nervous laughter that always preceded one of his revelations. "Her body doesn't threaten me the way Lo's did. And she's agreed to accept Jesus Christ in her life."

"What's Jesus got to do with it?"

"I could never go to bed with a girl who hasn't accepted Jesus into her life."

"And Lo wouldn't?"

"No," Alden said sadly.

What a mishmash! Alden and Patti Schmidt and Jesus Christ lying down in bed together, each bleeding from his own particular wounds. Quick, hand me a cross! Who's got the nails?

I walked in disbelieving silence into the kitchen. Alden got two glasses out of the drainer.

"Want some wine?"

"I need a drink after that."

He carried the glasses through the den. There was an upright piano with a hymnbook opened on the stand. More couches, more coverlets.

The liquor cabinet, it turned out, was the reverend's desk. Chuck opened the drawer to an enormous jug of sherry, a gallon or two of the real sweet stuff.

"Blood of the grape," he announced.

"Sounds like blasphemy. I thought you weren't supposed to talk like that."

"You Jews are so particular about your religion!" he teased me. "Even ones who don't believe."

"We have to be particular. Especially ones who don't believe."

Alden set the glasses on his father's ecclesiastical blotter and filled them with sherry. It tasted like Robitussin with dextra-mophorathan.

"You haven't seen the rest of the apartment." He pushed open another in the series of doors.

"The master bedroom! The bed of my procreators! Where it all happened!"

"I see two beds," I pointed out. "Which one did it happen in?"

"Neither. At the time they slept in the same bed."

He sat on one of the beds. Something I would never dare do in my parents' bedroom.

"You were with Patti, weren't you?"

"We tried."

"And so was I. We tried, and we succeeded." He was satisfied with himself. "You could say you and I touched inside her body."

I didn't want any part of it, not if that concentration-camp body was involved. "Nothing sexual could happen in that asexual being. We tried. But *we* didn't succeed."

Alden put both hands on the crocheted bedspread. "Don't *you* want to try? A girlfriend can't give you everything. There are friends too."

"I know that. It's just that I haven't agreed to accept Jesus Christ into my life."

"That's only for girls."

"Sounds like the Jesus flip-flop to me."

Alden jumped up. I think he'd surprised himself with his proposition.

"I wrote a song. I want you to listen to it."

I waited in the reverend's closed-in bedroom until Alden came back with his guitar. The only thing Chuck Alden could do without attaching a thousand qualifiers and backtracking was sing. And even then it was a song of censorship:

> Children know it isn't right
> You must never go down to the lake at night.

And his drowning children replied:

> Help me Lord I'm sinking down
> The water's rushing all over me.

He put his guitar down.

"I'm going to meet Mayo in the Hole. He wants to."

"Do you know what you're doing?"

"No."

"I think you do."

I SPENT THAT WEEK waiting around for something to give with Alden. Nothing happened. I had rejected him on his mother's bed and now he wouldn't talk to me. Meanwhile, Blowy got his notice telling him where and when to report for his medical and outlining the consequences if he did not report.

Something else happened: Yvonne Chezevski became a Kensington Krazy. She walked into the Blot one Friday night with two little gold stars stuck on either side of her green-blue eyes. I made room for her at our booth. When she saw she was welcome she took off the stars.

She came just in time for me. Now that Alden was with Patti Schmidt, I had begun to consider Lo. I had even convinced myself I liked the way she drooped her hair in the ashtray. I couldn't get my mind off the walls of the vagina. I pictured an enormous palace and me very small, like in *Gulliver's Travels*, in awe looking up at the shiny walls stretching heavenward.

Yvonne's good meat-on-the-bones sensuality put a stop to all that. I knew there would be something comforting to hold under those loose dresses she wore. She came from the Highlands, a Kensington euphemism, a subdivision of thin walls and no basements because if the contractors dug them, they would be filled with water before the first raindrop fell, the land was so marshy out there. She drew and painted a little. Her father was a policeman.

"He's not a narc and he's not in a patrol car. He's a detective. You'll never have to meet him," Yvonne promised me.

Like Lo and Patti Schmidt, Yvonne did not feel comfortable in her body. But she was not at war. Not badly enough to want to carve up her soft arms with her daddy's razor blade. Just uncomfortable enough to want a lot of reassurance. I could do that.

Blowy ordered a lemon-cream pie and coffee. We took turns reading his order to report for the medical. Blowy was the first person we knew who would be forced to have something to do with the war. It was like the war had finally come home, into our house, and Blowy was the one who had caught it. Patti Schmidt was taking a little sip of water after every one of Blowy's forkfuls of pie, like she was cleaning her precious little system. I felt like knocking the glass out of her hand.

"I like this life," Blowy said after the letter had made the rounds. "I'm a born landscaper. I'm good with sod. I'm not college material, you all know that. This is my country. It's only rotten at the top. That'll end soon."

Blowy was a good American: he thought best at the wheel of his car. We paid and decided to take a spin in Angel. As we left the table I saw Patti wheel around and grab a half-crust of lemon-cream pie and stuff it in her mouth.

Blowy got Angel out of the Friday-night traffic and onto Ogden Avenue where it crossed the Forest Preserve. We drove past a landfill site and up over the Tri-State Expressway.

"Consider the alternatives," Flynn was telling Blowy.

Flynn was in back with Alden and Patti. Yvonne was with me in the front with Blowy.

"I'm considering them," Blowy said. "*Uno*: cop a C.O. I met a Quaker who did that. He shoveled shit for two years in a hospital in Alabama for the criminally insane. If I'm going to spend two years with the criminally insane, I might as well be in Vietnam. Anyway, I'm not going to go up in front of the Board and swear I'm a pacifist when all I want to do is bash their heads in."

"Visit another country," I suggested.

"*Due*: Canada. I don't even know where that is. It's cold up there all the time and they have French hockey players. Winter soldiers don't run away. This place belongs to me."

Flynn counted the options on his fingers. "Be a fag."

"Get serious. Do these hands look like fag hands? They look like landscaping hands."

"Get hurt—a little."

"A little's plenty enough. I know my Board—and it's your Board too. We fought, now you fight, a war's a war. A good Bohunk Board, squat and ugly and Ogden Avenue, like every-thing in this town. You think they're going to let me off for a hangnail? With our Board you've got to cut all the way to the bone. And I happen to like my fingers and toes. They go together real nice."

"Act crazy."

"I am, I am. I'm a Kensington Krazy. But that's not enough for them."

To show the invisible Board what he could do, Blowy stepped hard on the gas. A joint of throat-killing weed made the rounds.

Blowy was serving himself seconds on every go-round. The derelict trees of the Cook County Forest Preserve fell away more swiftly.

"What did the draft counselor say?" I felt it was going to be the last coherent question anyone asked.

"He wants to turn me into a five-year, ten-thousand-dollar man. Plain noncooperation. Turn me into an example. That's all right, that's his job. But I'm not pure enough to be anybody's example."

That was it. We began to sing the Kensington Krazy song:

> I'm a fool, yessirree
> I'm gonna die when I'm twenty-three—
> And always take your conscience for a ride!

There we were, a bunch of self-destructive hips in a V-8 automobile invented for people like us, perverting Jiminy Crickets. When the Man's heat turned up, the flower child wilted and the delinquent shone through.

"Let's go for a hundred," Blowy offered.

"You're at the wheel," I told him.

Yvonne held my hand. I kissed her and she was really there for me. Her mouth was dry from the grass and I wet her lips with my tongue. I looked up the road: it was coming in fast. I was glad that I was in the front seat, and that she was with me.

Flynn sang:

> I'm a fool, yessirree
> Don't look for me when you're twenty-three—
> And always let your unconscience be your guide!

"Maybe I just won't do anything at all." Blowy was talking in short spurts.

"You're going eighty-five miles an hour!" Alden reported, alarmed, from the back.

His eyes were wide. Patti's were closed. *Is she going to throw up?* I wondered.

"Not *you*," Flynn corrected Alden, "*we*. Anyway, it's ninety by now."

"If you don't do anything, it's like going." It sounded moral but I had to say it. I put my hand on Yvonne's breast. "If I'm gonna die on Ogden Avenue I want to die with my hands on a pretty girl's breasts."

She took my other hand and put it on her other breast. Our legs were moving faster than the rest of our bodies. It wasn't an unpleasant sensation. There was so much happening inside the car and out on the surface of the road that I didn't know where to look. Alden was squirming like a worm in the backseat and Flynn started elbowing him hard in the ribs to get him to calm down and not hurt Blowy's concentration. Patti Schmidt was practicing some kind of denial next to Alden.

"Maybe I'll enlist," Blowy was saying. "I'll get a better deal."

"Enlist? Enlist? Spit those words out!"

Then, real laconically, Blowy said, "Look, we're at a hundred. Good, good Angel, I knew you could do it."

He had reached the plateau and now he wanted to stay there. Very slow and calm, he said, "You know, I want to resist but I don't think I know how to. I feel real stupid trying to fight it. I just want to be free."

We were at the top of the Tri-State Bridge. Below on the expressway the cars crawled along at seventy or seventy-five. Flynn came in, real soothing.

"Blowy, there's a traffic light down there. See, at the end of the bridge. It's there so the cars coming off the Tri-State can get onto Ogden Avenue."

Yvonne pressed against me. Her fear was honest. I didn't want Blowy to take us over the edge this night, either. And not River Edge, where nothing happened and where you always came back from.

Then Blowy responded. He touched the brake once, twice, then hard. The Chevy fishtailed a little, a Detroit glider with only a passing acquaintanceship with the road surface. The cross traffic moved across our path ahead at the light, slow and unreal. We could have been flying over Ogden Avenue in an airplane. We weren't going to stop in time for the light. Everyone knew it. It was still red for us. Blowy leaned on the horn and flashed his lights. As he did Alden, goddamn him, let out a scream. Everything had been all right till then. And it stayed all right, at least as far as the outside world was concerned. The cross traffic held as the missile of noise and flashing light cut through the red.

Blowy was calm. He pulled off Ogden to make a U-turn back to Kensington.

"This is a bring-down."

He swung into traffic and went back up the Tri-State Bridge. "I only stopped because of you guys."

I FINALLY UNDERSTOOD what bothered me about Blowy. The singing aunts and uncles brought it home to me. That Sunday afternoon my parents had gone to a peaceful march around the federal building downtown, to protest the latest escalation. They went with those of the aunts and uncles who had not entirely sold themselves to bill collecting or other low forms of commerce. After the march they came home to the house for poppy-seed cake and weak coffee. It was hard imagining that the oldest among the aunts and uncles had helped make the revolution in another country. But they had.

The first piece of cake had an effect on them like strong drink. They started remembering, which was dangerous in some of their cases, considering what their memories might find. They remembered the relatives lost in Europe during the war, and how much they would have enjoyed a nice peaceful protest like the one this afternoon. In their stories, the relatives stood rooted and immobile as barns as they waited for the massacre to come to their settlement.

"Why didn't they do anything? Why did they just wait?"

The heavy heads of my aunts and uncles turned in my direction. My father glanced down. It was the wrong question to ask.

"You in America will do different next time," said my favorite uncle, who was a socialist shoe salesman, "for there *will* be a next time."

It was a good and noble answer. But when I thought of Blowy, in my own neighborhood, I could see we were not doing different.

I WAS ALONE WITH Yvonne. The night was still warm. Only we had no bed where we could lie down together.

We made all of Kensington our bed. Parks, backyards in the neighborhoods where people worked for a living. Where they went to bed early and slept hard from the bourbon in their systems.

At first you can't do it. You can sit down together, kiss and touch, then maybe lie down. But can you unzip your jeans and pull them over your knees and ankles and be ass naked in a stranger's postage-stamp backyard? Especially for a girl.

Yvonne began to wear skirts. Skirts and knee socks. It got to be a signal. Knee socks meant she wanted to. We found a trellis or a sheltered place under evergreens where there was no dew. In the neighborhoods where they work for a living, they like to fix their backyards. She slipped down her panties and put them in her purse. I only dared slip my jeans down over my ass. I wasn't really naked.

Then we got bolder. One time, it must have been one o'clock in the morning. The air was cool. I took off all my clothes. She pulled her dress over her head. I touched her between her legs and she was already wet there. I didn't understand much about it, but being inside her made me feel less lonely and less afraid about what would happen with Blowy and Alden. How we were letting go of Alden because he'd stopped being one of us, and how we couldn't stop Blowy from drifting into war. Yvonne and I were at our favorite place, with the rose trellis. We danced naked in some stranger's backyard. I crept around to the front and looked at the mailbox to see whose hospitality we were enjoying. Mr. Wrablik's. We rolled naked in the grass in Mr. Wrablik's backyard and I put the petals of his roses and tulips in all the spots you would expect on Yvonne's perfect, perfect body. The lights were on in Mr. Wrablik's house. We went to see what he was doing, if it was different from what we were doing. It was. He had fallen asleep in front of the television; there was a black-and-white movie playing. The dirt of his flower beds under our feet. We were naked in Kensington. We pretended it all belonged to us.

We went back to the trellis. I didn't know everything she felt when we made love. Once she tapped her belly and said, "I can feel it inside me." I took that as a good sign.

I would never live that pure again.

The Hole

3

We hadn't invented the Hole. We weren't even the first ones to use it. The Hole had been there ever since there had been a Kensington. It was part of the natural history of Kensington, and Kensington needed it.

The Hole was our free zone provided to us by water. To the north, west and east: the streets and sidewalks of the district of Kensington, all nicely laid out the way the wooden-house builders had wanted it. To the south: the Highlands, where Yvonne lived. Where the contractors had done something with worthless land, where on summer nights you could hear the motor maniacs revving up their engines on the clay track of the Santa Fe speedway. In the middle was the Hole, a giant unusable tract of land hostile even to developers. Making a mockery of property values. An underground stream kept the land in permanent sloppiness and miserable with mosquitoes. It was unreclaimable. Downtown Chicago had been built on garbage landfill; the glorious twin towers of Marina City rested on old tin cans. But the builders had not gotten to the Hole yet.

I called the meeting down there. I knew Charles Alden was going to have his little encounter with Mayo tonight. He had boasted about it long enough. He telegraphed it: watch me.

Blowy got Angel in on one of the hardened dirt tracks the developers who wanted to dump for free had made. Flynn sat on the hood, navigating, signaling to Blowy to cut left or right to avoid a muddy spot or a pointed rock. I was in front with Yvonne. Patti Schmidt had the whole backseat to herself.

The radio was on, Eric Burdon's hard, brooding voice. The Animals:

It's a hard world to get a break in
All the good things have been taken
But girl there's ways
To make certain things pay...

The sky was mercury-vapor orange, the color of rust inhibitor.

"I hate this place," Blowy said. "Angel hates it too."

Yvonne was tense. She was holding my hand but her hand was lifeless. It felt unclean in here.

Flynn was waving his arms on the other side of the windshield. "That's it," he called, "I'm not letting Angel go any further. We're gonna have to back out all the way as it is."

Flynn jumped down. We all got out.

"We should have walked," Patti said.

Flynn glared at her. "Where's Lo tonight?"

"Back at the Edge," I answered for Patti.

"What did she do now?"

"It's safer inside," Patti explained, as if she had a direct line to Lo's head. Who knows, maybe she did. She could keep it.

Flynn looked disgusted. I got out an imaginary violin. We weren't in the mood for candle-wax poetry tonight.

We sat on Angel's hood. Blowy left the key in the ignition so we could hear the radio. I could have told Patti Schmidt that was why we didn't walk in. It felt better sitting on Angel's silver fenders than on the swampy ground.

"All right, den mother," Flynn said to me. "You got us in here. Tell us why."

"You know why. Alden's gonna ruin things for us. I want us to stop him."

"Did you see him tonight?" Blowy asked.

"No. But I think I know where he's gonna be. He's supposed to meet Mayo tonight."

"He's fucked up," Flynn declared.

"We know that. But what are we going to do about it?"

Flynn looked irritated. "*Do*? What's to do? I already made up my mind. I'm not going to *do* anything about him. I'm going to turn him loose."

"Why are you so mad at him?"

That slowed down Flynn, which is what I wanted to do. "You know something, Rabb, you're right: I am mad at him. I'm mad at him because he's fucking up in a real obvious, unimaginative way when there's bigger problems to be concerned with, and we're all getting dragged into it, mostly through you, no offense, but because you seem to be his friend. I don't get his thing with Mayo and I don't want anything to do with it. Do you?''

"No, of course not. I tried to talk him out of it.''

"Talk, talk, talk,'' said Blowy: his analysis of the situation.

"But I can't see just letting him drop. He's one of us—''

"He *was*.''

"Look, just because he's doing one fucked-up thing, does that mean we get rid of him?''

"You want to save him,'' Yvonne said. In her voice it didn't sound like criticism. But it was.

"You want to save him from himself,'' Flynn said. "You should get a job at the Edge.''

Patti Schmidt let out a dry little laugh. "That's hilarious! Rabb at the Edge. He's too stable.''

"Look who's talking,'' Flynn shot back. "I suspect you've got hidden reservoirs of stability.''

"Talk, talk, talk,'' Blowy analyzed.

Flynn, to his credit, tried to get things back on track. "You're not letting him drop, anyway, not if you talked to him the way you said you did.''

"I sort of talked to him. I talked to him as much as anybody can.''

"Talk, talk, talk.''

"Make up your mind,'' Flynn told me. "Alden's trying to fuck with Mayo's mind—that is, if Mayo's got one. And since I'm not into mind fucking, and since I'm not into body drugs like dex, and since Alden doesn't have any dex anyway, and since none of us are into it, and since he knows that, let him do his own thing. I'm boycotting him.''

"But I don't know if he knows what he's doing.''

"That *is* the question,'' said Flynn, "isn't it?''

We all listened to the question under the unhealthy, wasted sky. An early-summer wind coming out of the southeast, over Stickney, the sewage plant, the paint factory. When we were kids and smelled that smell, we used to say, "The mouse that ate the rusty cheese.'' It was a rusty Limberger smell.

Flynn popped open a Stroh's and I jumped.

"Here—drink. We're celebrating."

"I'm not in the mood."

"Come on. Blowy's seen the light. He's staying on our side. He told me he's not joining the military-industrial complex after all. He told me he's not yet begun to fight."

Blowy was embarrassed. "I never told you that."

"You're right, you didn't." Flynn got serious. "I must have been dreaming."

"A nice dream," Yvonne said.

I took Flynn's beer, drank a sip or two and handed it to Yvonne.

"I think I'm going to take a walk. I know he's out there somewhere."

Yvonne got up with me. She set the bottle on Angel's fender. Against his better judgment Blowy followed. He was just looking for something to happen. Patti slipped in behind him, a gray smudge in the darkness.

Flynn stayed put on the Chevy hood. He picked up the beer and finished it in one long pull.

"You can't be two places at once."

He threw the bottle into a clump of bushes. There was a rock underneath and the bottle exploded.

"Remember Janie James," he called out after us.

THE DEVELOPERS' DUMP in the clearing had been psychedelicized. The broken concrete blocks all decorated with Day-Glo paint in wavy lines. That was not our work. There were other Krazies out here in the Hole.

I was leading and I saw Charles Alden alone in the middle of the tamped mud clearing. I spotted him just before we burst through the brush to where he stood. Before it was too late. I did not want him to see me. Like I was ashamed. I wanted to keep a safe distance. It was uncool, following him like that. We weren't letting him do his own thing.

We would hang back and watch. Just in case.

He did not hear us. The four of us crouched in the bushes, spiderwebs in our hair, the mud soft under our feet. It was like a game of Swamp Fox. We didn't have to ask ourselves what we were doing. We were hiding; that was part of the game. I wondered what Alden was thinking out there. Was he going to tell Mayo about Jean Genêt? He must have been thinking how he was having a real experience. It must have been called fear and self-disgust.

Then Mayo showed and Weaver was with him. Now it was too late to do anything but listen and watch. Alden's machine was in motion.

Alden got up from the pile of stones he was sitting on. He tried to work it so he was facing Mayo and not Weaver. Mayo was rocking back and forth on his heels like he always did. He was a head taller than Alden. They stood facing each other. Now what?

"Ducks and bunnies?" Alden said.

Then he began to laugh. He couldn't help himself. The waiting must have made him hysterical. The only way he could calm down was to talk.

"I don't know why you want that shit anyway, it's not good for you." As if he actually had any to deal in the first place. "There's a lot better ways to get high, man. Get high on music. Get high on all this."

He looked up at the sky glowing orange and green, the lights of downtown Chicago bouncing off a bank of low clouds. Was Alden appealing to the heavens?

His voice rose. "Look, Tom, I've made you come all the way out here for nothing. Here you are, you've come out here for your little white pills that will make you feel like you're somebody and I don't have a thing to offer you."

"Just give him the shit," Weaver cut him off.

"Yeah, just give me the shit," Mayo echoed.

Alden turned on Weaver. "Aren't you listening? I just said I don't have any. You don't have anything to do with this, anyway. This is between Tom and I."

Alden's talk snapped something inside Mayo's head. "You woman!" he cursed him. With a quick uppercut he hit Alden under the chin and drove his teeth into his tongue and lips. He got another punch in but it did not count for much because Alden was falling away.

Yvonne clutched my hand. None of us moved. I was expecting it. That was how I thought it would end. Mayo stood over him. "Get up, you fucking woman!" But Alden would not get up.

His mouth was bleeding a little. Mayo kicked him in the ass, but not too hard. He must have been disappointed. It was not much of a fight.

Then Weaver finished it. We weren't expecting that. He picked up a big piece of broken concrete with psychedelic paint on it and crashed it down on Alden's head as he lay there. It was that fast. There was no time. Alden did not have a chance. It made a wet, sickening, vegetable sound.

"*You're* the woman," Weaver told Mayo. "Go get a shovel and bury him. Or take him home if you want to. He's yours."

"I'll get a shovel," Mayo promised him.

Then Weaver was gone. Mayo got down on his hands and knees and rolled Alden under a clump of bushes on the other side of the clearing from us. Then he ran to get his shovel. We were the only ones left.

And we were whispering, because the body was so near. "I never thought it would end like this." I think I was apologizing to the others. "I figured something would happen but not like that."

"Holy fuck, it was like a dream," Blowy said. "I watched it but I didn't believe it. It wasn't real. Otherwise I would have done something."

"We're in now," Yvonne moaned, "we're really in now."

"I don't want to be in. I want to be out. I want to be free." Blowy was whimpering.

It was crazy, but we were paralyzed. Alden was fifty feet away. Nobody wanted to go and see what we had let be done. It took Patti Schmidt to wake us up.

"He's alive," she began to whisper. "He's alive, I know he's alive."

"He can't be, not after that," Blowy told her.

Then Patti burst out of our hiding place. She was through the thicket faster than any of us and I felt a bramble branch whiz past my face as I followed her. She ran across the clearing for Alden's body and I saw the thorns had caught her across the cheek.

"Don't touch him!" I ordered her.

I didn't care who heard. She threw herself down next to Alden's body. When I got up next to her with Yvonne, I realized I didn't have to tell her that. No one would want to touch Chuck Alden's face or head now.

"He's alive, he's alive." Patti kept denying what she saw.

Then her voice rose. She screamed it. Blowy crossed behind her and clamped his palm over her mouth. I had visions of every delinquent in the Hole bursting into the clearing and finding us over Alden's corpse.

"Get her out of here, let's get her out of here. We'll take her back to the car. Then we'll see."

I motioned toward Alden, then I grabbed Patti's legs. Blowy had the top half of her body. There was no trouble carrying her back through the brush to Angel. We'd lay her down. Drive her somewhere. Home. A hospital. The Edge.

We sat her on the backseat. Flynn was lying on Angel's hood, accumulating empty bottles of Stroh's. He rolled off the hood and landed on his feet.

"Another freak-out?"

"Flynn, Alden got killed."

"Why, you stupid motherfuckers! I told you—"

"Shut up, Bobby," Blowy said softly. "It's done. We're into containment."

He nodded at Patti, then took his hand away from her mouth. She looked up at us as if everything was normal.

"I'm just telling you he's alive."

"We'll go see," Yvonne put in. "But what are we going to *do*?"

"I don't know, I don't know," I told her. "It all happened too fast."

Then Blowy answered. His voice was cool. "I'm short for Kensington. This isn't my place. You guys figure it out."

"Don't say 'short,' " Flynn begged him, "that's Army talk."

"So it is, so it is. Alden did what he wanted to. Nobody thought it was going to turn out like that."

"We didn't do anything," Yvonne moaned, "there wasn't anything to do until it was too late. Oh, shit, I don't want to be here!"

"You won't be," I promised her softly. "Only don't say we didn't do anything. I tried to talk him out of it."

We looked at each other and she shook her head. We both

knew that wasn't the point. We had let him go once. Now we were letting him go for good. Out of shame.

I turned to Patti Schmidt. "Do you want to go to the police?"

"The police?" She gave me one of her quizzical looks that made you think you were the crazy one.

"Forget it."

That was the best we would get from her.

Yvonne nudged me. "We'd better go and see."

"I'll stay here and help," Blowy said.

Yvonne and I pushed through the thicket. It seemed like a long way back to the clearing. When we came up to the edge we saw Alden still lying on the ground. People crisscrossed through the Hole all night long. Maybe someone had come this way. If they had they probably would have kept walking.

Then somebody did come. It was Mayo; this time he was alone. He had a shovel and a can. He started scraping a trench in the soft ground. It did not take long. He was in a hurry. He rolled Alden in and as he did we heard a sound. I almost threw up: Alden was still alive. Mayo started shoveling dirt. The grave was not deep enough. He just barely managed to cover Alden. Then he began to strip. He took off his shoes, his shirt, everything with Alden's blood on it. He squirted barbecue starter from a pressurized can and lit the pile. The flames rose up. There was a bad smell: his gym shoes had caught. The smoke drifted across the Hole. A few minutes later Mayo walked out of the clearing shirtless, in his socks, a shovel on his shoulder. He was a free man. All of Kensington looked the other way as he went home.

YVONNE PROMISED ME I would never have to meet her father, the sergeant-detective. She was wrong. But it wasn't really her fault.

At nine o'clock the next morning, May Alden was on the phone. Her voice was wispy, sincere, concerned. But not as worried as it could have been. "Vincent, my boy Charles didn't come home last night. He wouldn't be at your house, would he?"

"No."

"Were you with him last night?"

I told her I hadn't been.

"Can you do me a favor?"
"Sure."
"Come over."
"Come over?"
"Yes . . . if you don't mind."
How could I mind? When I got there, the reverend came out of his room. Sunday morning and he wasn't at work. I had never seen the reverend in the flesh before. He was compact and square-shouldered, like in the photo. He had one of those baby faces that English people sometimes have, and that baby face had been up all night wrestling with its demons. When you know something about someone, and they don't know you know, you just don't want to be around them.

May Alden was dressed for gardening. She had on a man's checked lumberjack shirt and ladies' jeans. A pair of gardening gloves stuck out of her back pocket.

The Aldens looked as though they were waiting for someone.

"Did you call the police?" I asked.

"Yes," May Alden said hesitantly. "It was the Reverend Alden's idea."

I tried to imagine the Reverend Alden's bare, hairy ass up in the air, pumping away inside the Kensington Presbyterian Church. It was a way to get my mind off current events.

Then company came. It was Sgt.-Det. Lewis Chezevski. I looked at his Bohunk cop's belly and his tired blue eyes and his Sunday-morning painting-the-garage clothes. You could tell he wished he were somewhere else. Me too.

There were handshakes all around.

"I asked Vincent to come over," May Alden said. "He's one of Chuck's best friends and . . . I don't know."

The detective looked disinterested. That must have been his method.

"Chuck didn't come home last night. I'm afraid something might have happened."

"And you waited until now." Chezevski stated the obvious.

"Chuck is a very . . . independent boy. A little agitated too, sometimes. He has to find his own way."

I could not believe May Alden was talking this way to a cop.

"Agitated?" he asked.

"My son's a bit of a poet," she said proudly. "Sometimes he stays out late at night, just walking . . . thinking. I go to bed early and get up at dawn. I'm the opposite from him."

Not so opposite, I thought, and maybe Chezevski thought the same way. Then an amazing thing happened: the Reverend Alden, who had not sat down, turned and walked out of the room without saying a word. May Alden blushed a little. Chezevski tried not to notice.

"When did you realize your son hadn't come back?"

"This morning, around eight-thirty."

"But you said you get up early."

"His door was closed," May Alden said, "I thought he was sleeping. We respect closed doors in this house."

Chezevski nodded. Underneath he looked disgusted. Then it was my turn to get a question.

"Do you know where he could have been last night?"

"No."

"Were there any parties he could have gone to?"

"If there were, we weren't invited."

"He wasn't with you last night."

"No, sir."

"Who were you with?"

I gave the names: Blowy and Flynn and Patti. I left out his daughter.

"If you want we'll help look for him."

Chezevski looked interested. "Where would you look?"

"If he went to a party we don't know about and got drunk and fell asleep, there's nothing we can do. Otherwise I'd look in the parks. In the Hole."

"The police patrol the parks. They would have seen him."

"If you say so. Then the Hole."

We all stood around for a moment. Then Chezevski said all right.

I got on the phone in May Alden's kitchen. It was all tidy except for a half-eaten pack of oatmeal cookies on the counter with crumbs spilling out. The reverend's breakfast. They actually had a God Bless This House knitted thing on the wall. I'd missed it last time. Arts and crafts.

I called Carl Stotl. That was part of the plan. He was a long-haired goof who didn't know how deep Alden was into the Mayo thing. An innocent. He agreed right away to help look for Alden.

Then I called up Blowy's. Flynn was over there too.

I went back to the living room. "Everybody wants to help," I reported. "They're coming over."

"We'll wait outside," Chezevski said.

He must have been as much in a hurry to get out of there as I was. We stood on the front step together. He turned and looked at the Alden house.

"I don't know why those people don't pull up their blinds. It's morning."

I shrugged. What was I supposed to say? That it was because they were weird? When the police are around you have to play dumb, and the police had never been this close. Maybe it was because he was Yvonne's father, but I got the feeling he wanted to talk. About the Alden household. About the pact that set Charles and his mother against the old man, mother and son, both sensitive in that anxious sort of way, chasing him out of the house to somewhere else where he could prove he was a man. I looked up and considered the new leaves on the trees, those that had not yet been hit by Dutch elm. I would be glad when this was over. When they found the body and started looking for the murderer, who obviously was not us.

Blowy drove by in Angel. Flynn and Stotl were with him in the front seat.

"If you don't want to look in the parks," I said to the Sgt.-Det., "we'll go out to the Hole. We'll meet you there."

May Alden materialized on the front step behind us. "I would like to go with you."

"You ride with Mrs. Alden," the cop instructed me.

We drove over to the Hole. A weird convoy on an ordinary Sunday morning in Kensington. Only the comforting drone of lawn mowers was missing. But it was a little too early for that.

The Alden family station wagon had a three-on-the-tree gear-shift. There was no radio. A cross swung from the rearview mirror. The reverend had written down the mileage for the next oil change and taped it to the dash.

"I know you judge us," May Alden suddenly said.

I wasn't in the mood for a surrealistic conversation, but it looked as though I had no choice. My instructions were to ride with May Alden.

"I don't judge you."

"Yes, you do. You judge us. I can feel it."

"I don't."

"You do. You judge, you judge." She was saying it half to herself.

"Okay, okay." I gave in. I felt weary, even if it was only nine-thirty in the morning. "I judge you, I judge you."

It was happening again: we were getting out-crazied. We thought the Kensington Krazies were the craziest thing around, then along came Mayo and Weaver. We thought we were having a real sincere rebellion; our parents turned out to be loonier than anything we could come up with. I had a flashback to when I was young: why don't adults just leave me alone? It was the same thing now, mothers making their daughters mother them and leaving them no taste for ever becoming women themselves. Insisting on granting their children freedoms they couldn't possibly know what to do with. Why didn't they admit they were parents and solve their problems out of our earshot?

May Alden took her eyes off the road and looked at me. "Judge not lest thou be judged." Colorless eyes delivering Scripture.

Then the Angel of Death came wheeling overhead, as real now as in my first nightmares. "Vengeance is mine, saith the Lord," I reminded her, my God against hers. So far mine was leading.

Then I smiled. "There's the Hole. Pull up behind the cop car."

An unmarked car was already at the site. Then Angel, with Blowy and Flynn and Stotl still inside. Then Chezevski's car. We parked in back of it. A cop I had not met came over to May Alden. She rolled down her window.

"Mrs. Alden, I'm Officer Travers. Maybe you'd better wait up here."

Then Blowy and Flynn and I did a slow-motion pick play at the edge of the Hole, like defenders on the basketball court. I moved away from May Alden's car and looked like I didn't know what to do. Then I crossed and picked up Blowy as he got out of Angel. Stotl was with Flynn on the passenger side. Then Flynn crossed in front of the car and picked up Blowy from me, and I got Stotl. Then I was ready to play.

Chezevski turned to us. "Any of you boys ever done a search before?"

We all shook our heads.

He was about to give us directions on the proper way to conduct a search, but he changed his mind. He didn't take us seriously.

"Just don't get too far apart. And walk in a straight line."

I looked back. May Alden was standing next to her car. Her hand was flat on the hood of the station wagon. She was gazing at a point just over our heads. Then we climbed down the four- or five-foot drop off the roadway and went into the Hole.

I felt the humidity coming up through my gym shoes right away. Walking in a straight line was a joke. The bushes were so thick it would take a machete to cut through. We followed the paths that ran through the brush, from clearing to clearing. I had never been in the Hole during daylight. I had never looked at what was lying on the ground. Heaps of scrap metal, a car door. Cold camp fires in the clearings with the smell of doused wood, prophylactics hanging from the bushes. Two blown-up rubbers on the ground, and two squeezed-out tubes of airplane glue next to them. A transistor radio that someone had stomped, with the guts rusting away. I felt something for Alden, horror, that he had to be in this unclean ground.

Blowy and Flynn were on separate paths. I had stayed with Stotl. The cops were behind us. They did not seem too comfortable in the Hole.

We walked from clearing to clearing, seeing nothing, brushing the spiderwebs away, scuffing at the ground, acting like a bunch of goofs. Finally we got to the water tower on the far side of the Hole. We leaned against the fence that surrounded it and waited for the cops to catch up. Stotl was busy brushing elm seeds out of his hair. The cops came through the line of bushes and into sight. Judging from the belly on Chezevski and the distasteful way they picked up their feet, they must have spent most of the time inside their cars.

"We didn't see anything," Blowy said.

"I never knew this place was so big," Flynn complained. "I don't mind looking some more but we need more people."

"Do you really think the Alden boy could be in here?" Chezevski asked him.

Flynn shrugged. "He could be. You said he couldn't be in the parks. He might be down on Wells Street."

"Could he have run away from home?"

"Naw," I said. "Nothing to run away from."

That put me in Chezevski's good graces. "Is there a lot of...experimenting that goes on in here?"

We all looked innocent. "Experimenting?" I asked.

"Yeah, you know..." Chezevski just could not say what he meant.

"Drug use," Travers finished for him.

"We don't go down here too much," I told him. "We're not too popular."

"Yeah," Stotl piped up. "If you got long hair, they want to pound the shit out of you."

"Disgusting," Chezevski said. Then he asked Travers, "How many men could we put on this?" The Kensington policemen were probably busy mowing their lawns. Chezevski didn't want to risk disturbing them.

"We've got lots of friends," Blowy volunteered, "but we need to get to a phone."

"We can radio in the names and numbers." They went tramping off across the field with Flynn in the lead, moving double time. Stotl and I did not even try to keep up. When we got back into the thick part of the Hole I told Stotl, "Let's go this way. I think we missed this path."

I let him go around me, guiding him from behind. We crossed the track where Blowy's car had been last night. *All right*, I thought, *you long-haired hippie goof with a name that sounds like a nickel bouncing down a sewer pipe—fetch!* And the poor bastard did. I felt bad for him. We made it into the clearing where Alden had been killed.

Stotl checked out the rocks splashed with Day-Glo paint. "Wow, man, welcome to the fun house." The tree trunks had wavy lines running down them like barber poles. I had not seen that last night. "This must be where the freaks hang out," Stotl said.

"Yeah. Freaks."

There was a foot sticking out of the ground. I saw it before Stotl did. I stuck my fist in my mouth.

"Wow, what's this?" He saw it too, all in wonderment. Life

was a dream, life was a scream. For me it was worse the second time.

"Wow, these people must have buried a mannequin, crazy freaks." Stotl pulled on the leg with the desert boot at the end. The boot let loose. Stotl stared down at the little downy red hairs and toenails. No mannequin has that, right, Stotl?

"Holy motherfuck!" He dropped the shoe and sat down in the dirt. "That can't be him..."

I could hear the revolt of his guts from where I stood, twenty feet away. He began to wail. "I touched it! I touched it!"

He went tearing through the Hole toward Gilbert Avenue where the cars were parked. He lost one of his shoes too. We wanted somebody innocent to find Alden and that's what we got. You can never imitate innocence. That's what I found out that morning.

I ran after him. I felt bad for Stotl, but the thing had taken on its own logic, starting when we hid in the bushes last night. Or starting before then, who knows?

Stotl ran across Gilbert Avenue, pointing, dancing up and down. He could not speak. I wished him nice dreams.

"Where? What?"

Chezevski had to bear hug Stotl to calm him down. Travers took the radio.

"Cancel the search," he called in. "We found the object."

"Just take me there," Chezevski told Stotl.

Stotl led. We followed. I heard May Alden calling, "Officer, officer," her voice rising with worry. Chezevski and Travers did not turn around.

In the clearing Stotl pointed. The desert boot was on its side on the ground. The foot sticking up like it was trying to climb out, the hem of a pair of jeans. "I touched it, I touched it," Stotl repeated. He had his hands over his eyes, like he was trying not to see anymore.

"Why? Why did you touch it?" Chezevski questioned him.

"I don't know, I thought it was some kind of joke."

"Joke? Is this your idea of a joke?" Chezevski was disgusted.

"People do those kind of things here," I defended Stotl. He was in no shape to do it himself. "They bury mannequins, you know, for a joke."

"That ain't no mannequin," Travers summed up.

Chezevski looked irritated. He kicked aside some of the loose dirt around the leg. Alden's blue jeans. Alden's desert boot. Chezevski was taking it pretty hard too. Maybe he was thinking of what to tell May Alden.

"Listen carefully now," he said to us. "Go back to your houses and don't say a thing about what you saw. Say you didn't see anything if anyone asks you—even your parents. I'll be coming around to talk to you later. I don't want any rumors being spread, or anything that might tip off whoever killed this boy."

We nodded. We understood. We walked out of the Hole, past May Alden, without even looking at her. That was the hardest part.

I opened the door of Blowy's car for Stotl.

"I think I'm going to walk," he said. "I could use the air. Shit, if I ever thought I was going to find something, I wouldn't have searched."

It was a weird thing for Stotl to say, but I understood. It was like one of those Zen sayings, but backwards somehow.

"I'll call you up tonight," I promised him. "We'll get together. We'll talk."

He walked away.

We drove down Gilbert Avenue, Blowy and Flynn and I in the front seat.

"First Alden," Blowy said, "then we fuck with Stotl."

"He did a good job," Flynn said. "I'm glad I wasn't there when it happened. I saw all I needed to see this morning."

"But you *were* there, Flynn," I told him.

Blowy looked at his hands on the steering wheel. "We're just driving around," he said. "I want to go someplace but there isn't anywhere to go."

"That's a sign it's time to go home," Flynn said.

I felt like walking too. I asked Blowy to let me off.

"You guys got your stories all right?" I asked before I got out.

"Sure, boss."

"Just remember," I told them, "we didn't kill Chuck Alden."

"PATTY SMITH WAS RIGHT," Yvonne said. Her voice was low even though there was nobody around. "He died of suffocation. You know what that means?"

"No."

"He was alive when he was buried, just like Patti said. He breathed in the dirt. He suffocated from that. That's how he died!"

"But we didn't know that then."

She pulled a bud off Mr. Wrablik's rosebush and threw it on the ground. One less flower.

"I'm not accusing you of anything, so don't defend yourself."

"Sorry, just a bad habit. Did your father tell you how he died?"

"He *never* talks about cases. This one is different. He was telling my mother and I sort of overheard. He talks in Czech but he forgets I understand."

"He looked pretty disgusted in the Hole. And before, too."

"He is. He couldn't believe the Aldens. He's big on family love and everything. He practically blamed them for their kid getting killed. Then he said he couldn't keep up with the violence any more. I think the walk through the Hole freaked him out."

"An innocent policeman. It's hard to imagine."

"I know. It's strange, but that's the way he is. 'The happiest man on the force'—that's what they call him at work. Not any more, I guess. He went back to the station after you guys found Alden and read your files. The narcs have reports on everyone they think smokes grass. Of course my name was in there too."

"Oh, shit."

"That's all right, he doesn't take those files seriously anyway. He said they were as useful as a report on everyone in Kensington who used the word 'fuck.' "

We laughed. It felt good to. I took her in my arms and we fell back on the grass. The soft earth, on our side. May the dead spin in their graves, but I did not want to lose Yvonne over this.

"You know what else he said? He was reading the narco files and there was something about you guys consuming controlled substances in a public park, and how the police confiscated the substances, which had a street value of a $1.99."

"Two six-packs of Drewry's!"

"Right! And my father said, 'Hey, I missed that sale!' "

And we laughed again, a little too loud, and I was afraid we'd

wake up Mr. Wrablik crashed out in front of the TV set. I pulled
Yvonne on top of me. She's a healthy girl and I'm all skin and
sinews like any good cross-country runner, I felt a little over-
whelmed, but I undid her shirt and found her breasts. When I
grow up, I thought, if that ever happens, I'm gonna have this all
the time.

"I don't know if we should."

"We'll do it for Alden."

"He wouldn't approve."

"He's a queer spirit anyway. Poor bastard, kicking around
down there."

"He tried to claw his way up. That's what my daddy says."

"Just let me stay up here with you."

The Angel of Death went wheeling away in crazy circles when
we made love under Mr. Wrablik's rose trellis. But he was never
far. Just temporarily disabled. We would not dance on the lawn
afterwards, like last time. Kensington did not belong to us like
before.

"Physical evidence," Yvonne breathed. "My father found all
kinds of burned stuff from the fire Mayo made. He's gonna have
it analyzed. Then he's gonna ask you guys some questions."

I GOT MY VISIT from the Sgt.-Det. the next day. The Joliet Crime
Lab must have worked overtime to give Chezevski his data. I
was first on the list of visits, then Blowy, Flynn and Patti Schmidt.
I did not think we would hold our stories and there was a moment
when I didn't care. But when the authorities sat down across
from me, I swung back into the game.

"You were best friends with Alden," Chezevski told me.

I nodded.

"What kind of person was he?"

"Jesus Christ, that's a question!"

"Don't you want to answer it?"

"I'd like to, but it's a little complicated."

"And why is that?"

"There was more than one Alden." I was trying to explain it
to myself as I explained it to the cop. "On one hand he was real

sensitive, he could play music and sing, none of us could do that. On the other hand he was into head-tripping people."

Chezevski squinted. He did not understand. We really did talk a different language.

"He liked to play games with people's heads—with their minds," I explained.

"I see." Did Chezevski really see? "Could that have gotten him into trouble?"

"It could have. If he head-tripped the wrong person."

"How would that work?"

The policeman got real interested. It was a headtrip in itself. I was going to point him in Mayo's direction. If not in Mayo's precise direction, at least someone like him.

"Well, nobody likes to be head-tripped, right? So if he head-tripped the wrong person, then that person would get mad at him."

"Mad enough to kill him?"

"I don't know anybody who would. That's not our style."

"Whose style? Hippie style?"

I couldn't help laughing. "Hippies!" Let him think we were hippies. Everybody knew that hippies loved each other. They wore love beads and held hands. They didn't hit people over the head with large pieces of pavement.

"Okay, okay, so you're not hippies. I don't know who is and who isn't," he confessed. "I just know what it looks like to me. Anyway, you're telling me that the Alden boy could have head-tripped someone who might have reacted violently enough to kill him. Were you with him that night?"

"No."

"Where were you?"

"In Gilbert Park."

"A block from where the Hole starts."

I didn't say anything. We both knew our Kensington geography.

"It was Saturday night. You hung out with Alden. Why wasn't he with you then?"

"He must have had something else to do."

"What?"

"I don't know."

"Wasn't that a little unusual? Aren't you supposed to be best friends?"

"It was unusual," I conceded. "Charles was doing something, or being with somebody, and he wasn't telling me."

"Could he have told anybody else?"

I shrugged. "Maybe Patti Schmidt. They were going out together."

That must have been the end of the interview. He got up. "We'll be talking again," he promised.

There was something I liked about Chezevski. His being up against something so foreign to him.

"I wished I did understand more about Alden," I told him.

"Call me if something comes to mind. You know, son, we have a special relation."

"Yvonne," I said.

"Yes. My daughter. My only child."

Then he left.

OVER THE PHONE, Yvonne reported, "He asked me what a head-trip was."

"What did you tell him?"

"I said it was when one guy, who's smarter than another guy, tries to put something over on him."

"I think he head-tripped me. Right at the end."

Yvonne didn't ask what about. "He's a lot smarter than people give him credit for."

Proud of papa.

WAY SOUTH OF KENSINGTON, past the Highlands, is the Illinois and Michigan Shipping Canal. A tall, graceful metal bridge spans it, with a smooth concrete embankment under the bridge that slopes gently toward the water. A place to pull your car off the road. An unincorporated area, unpoliced. A canal dug through the marsh. A few sand barges use it, that's all. The setting for a Friday night Kensington Krazy picnic.

Blowy and Flynn, Yvonne and me, and Patti Schmidt. And Carl Stotl, who was going to discover that he'd been used by his fellow freaks. Hardly any traffic on the bridge overhead. The concrete embankment had a nice easy slope, you could lie down on it if you wanted to. As long as you didn't lie down sideways. Then you would roll into the canal.

"Let this Krazy picnic begin," I declared.

"No more picturesque spot," Flynn agreed. "Call the shots, den mother."

"Did everybody say the same thing to Mr. Policeman?"

"I did a hippie number on him," Blowy went first. "I said the vibrations were all wrong. He started doing his own thing without us. We didn't hassle him or nothing like that. I didn't know what he was into down in the Hole. Jesus Christ! I fucking hate that kind of talk! I hated hearing myself talk like that, all clued out."

"Flynn?"

"More or less the same. Less hippie-dippy. I didn't know him too good. He wasn't my style, too much of a brain. I couldn't imagine who would want to do something like that. It didn't seem like him—he wasn't a fighter, he wasn't a lover... At least I could swear I didn't see him that night."

"Okay, okay." I turned to Patti, our weak link. But not that weak, or we would not have been sitting under the bridge tonight.

Patti's recital was like being at the freak show. "The officer was very nice to me. I told him Chuck had become strange to me lately. He didn't talk to me the way he used to. He didn't show me his poems. He didn't desire me the way he used to. He used to want to touch me, you know, then he said he couldn't any more. His God didn't allow it." Then, real trusting, real innocent: "I didn't know anything about this new God of his. After all, he was the first one who ever . . . who was ever inside my body. He made me bleed. I said he could do it once a month, when I had my period. But then I stopped having my period."

"You told the police all this?"

"Oh, yes! The officer knocked over the chair on his way to leave."

"I wonder why."

"Don't worry, den mother," Flynn said to me, "she's the safest bet of any of us."

"You mean Alden got killed and you know something about it you're not saying? What's going on?" Finally Stotl caught on to what was happening around him. Then it flashed on him, as

it would have to, listening to us. "You didn't . . . you didn't
kill him, not you guys!"

He looked as though he wanted to jump up and run down the
embankment and throw himself into the canal to escape us. I put
my arm on his shoulder.

"Take it easy, Stotl, do you think we'd kill Chuck Alden? We
happened to be down in the Hole and we saw something, but
we're just not talking about it."

"Hey, den mother," Flynn said, "he thinks we did it. That's
funny!"

"You can't blame him," I told Flynn, "there was a minute
there when I was sitting down with Chezevski and I actually
thought I did do it. I had this flash: *should I confess?*"

"Would you tell me what's going on?" Stotl looked panicked.

"What's going on," said Flynn, "is the stupidest dog-and-
pony show in the whole circus. Vinnie here wanted to save Alden
from himself, he wanted to do his Elephant-Ears number, but
instead he dragged all of us—except me, but I might as well have
been there—into a scene where Tom Mayo and his friend were
bashing in Alden's head."

"You're covering for Tom Mayo? Holy shit!"

"You'd have to be there to understand," I said, using the old
line.

"You guys got bad vibrations!"

"Zipper up, freak, and smoke this," Blowy told Stotl. "When
you've had a toke we'll tell you the whole wild story."

Stotl took a great big toke. I think we all did. I was still trying
to keep the smoke down when the shit hit me. This was no Wisco
weed.

"What is this stuff?"

"Ah! Aha! I'm glad you asked that question." Blowy was
triumphant. Stoned victorious. "Joss sticks. Got it from a buddy.
Apparently it's dirt cheap in Nam."

"Nam. Blowy, that's Army talk." I was very far away from
my thoughts. They refused to lie end to end like they usually
did. I had to leap with them. "It's Alden, right, Blowy? That's
why you're going."

"Fuck all this Alden shit, I'm tired of it. Fuck Alden."

"You can't. He's dead," Flynn put in.

Stotl had the joint. He looked at it like it was a turd he was smoking. "Get this shit away from me." He half threw it at Blowy, who barely managed to save it from rolling down the embankment into the canal. "Would you please tell me what's going on?"

I put my finger into the air like a preacher or someone testing the wind. I heard a sand barge hoot somewhere down the canal. "We are not men of reflection. We don't usually answer straight questions..."

"Or questions from straights," Flynn intoned. For all our differences we both knew talk was a form of craziness.

"But you should know two things: we did not kill Charles Alden. And if we are covering for anyone, we are covering for ourselves."

"The guilt complex—you've heard of it?"

"Because we let him do what he wanted to do so bad, which was to go down to the Hole with Mayo and his friend the Weaver, with not a single cap of dex to placate him, and try to fuck with Mayo's mind, which turned out to be the mind of an ordinary maniac..."

"And then, to our silent dismay..."

"We came upon Mayo and Alden in the Hole since we just happened to be down there, half involved you could say, and we didn't rush into the clearing where they were, howling and waving our arms to scare away Mayo, or something like that..."

"We hid, and we watched..."

"And unfortunately Alden got killed."

"And so it was," Flynn finished.

"You would have had to have been there," Yvonne said.

And so ended the Kensington Krazy funeral oration for Chuck Alden, pronounced on Vietnam weed. Then the barge hooted again and it was right there on top of us, or at least it felt that way. The thing had a kind of searchlight on the front and it was sweeping the banks of the canal, the siren calling loud and hollow under the bridge, the propellers churning up a foam of foul detergent in the water. We were caught in the searchlight. Patti Schmidt froze, her victim eyes all wide and her shadow behind her a poor, ghostly thing. Blowy hit the ground and started to roll like the soldier he wanted to be. I was afraid he'd roll all the way down to the canal and I threw myself on him. The barge engine and siren made an incredible roar and echo under the bridge, our ears screamed and begged for it to pass, so loud we could say anything we wanted and not be heard. Flynn began yelling the grossest obscenities, and it was the instant of relief we needed in that storm of noise. I yelled, "I didn't do it, I didn't do it," and Yvonne, my Yvonne got crazy too, and I realized that girls were just as crazy as we were and it wasn't true they were going to protect us from ourselves and lead us out of this to a softer, quieter life. Yvonne was hollering, "Who killed Chuck Robin? Who killed Chuck Robin?" Blowy was screaming as loud as he could: "I know who killed Alden! I killed Chuck Robin? Who killed Chuck Robin?" Blowy was screaming as loud as he could: "I know who killed Alden! I killed Alden! I killed Alden!" Someone is really going to hear him, I thought, this is no game. The barge was moving out from under the bridge and Blowy was the only one standing when everyone else was in the trench with their heads down. "I killed . . . I killed . . ." Blowy's voice echoing under the bridge and no more barge noise to cover it.

"It's a bad trip," Blowy moaned.

"You can't bad trip on grass." It was the only time I saw Flynn be rough on Blowy.

"It's Vietnam grass," Blowy defended himself, "it's like a warning."

"That's all right," I told him, "we got plenty of that shit here. If you want to fight a war, you don't have to cross the ocean."

It looked as though the meeting was over. There was no chance of calling it back to order. We had lost the rule book. We scrambled up the side of the hill to the roadway where Blowy's car was.

Another car passed slowly over the bridge and we waited for it to go by.

"That's my daddy's car," Yvonne said real soft.

Right ahead of us an Olds 88 glided by. Inside, all glassy and moonlike and inquiring, was the face of Sgt.-Det. Chezevski.

Another silent, understated, but effective head-trip by the Sgt.-Det. Yvonne was caught in the middle. She was proud of her daddy, she wanted him to solve the case. But she wanted him to do it without involving her or me. I did not see how that could be.

We got into Angel. Nobody said a word. Blowy did not even

turn on the radio. It was a combination of that withdrawn feeling you can get on good grass and the Sgt.-Det.'s head-trip.

We moved toward the center of Kensington. Blowy drove like a stoned person drives: slowly, meticulously. Besides, he was holding.

"I feel like some lemon-cream pie," he said after a while.

"Maybe we shouldn't be seen together," Stotl said back.

"Crap," Flynn told him, "every cop in Kensington knows we hang out together. If we weren't together they'd think something was wrong."

"Anyway, I'm at the wheel," Blowy reminded Stotl.

It was a little thing for Blowy to say, but it said a lot. He had the wheel, he was going to tell us our destination. It was a power trip over Stotl, over the rest of us too. Blowy would never have said something like that before. Lemon-cream pie it was. We drove toward the Kensington main drag.

"I hear Lo is out of the Edge," Stotl said, trying for conversation. "Maybe we should go and get her at her place."

"I'm not in the mood for problem girls," Blowy replied. He turned around to Patti Schmidt, in the backseat with me and Yvonne. "Hey, Patti, let's say I buy you a nice big slice of pie, huh? Put some meat on your bones. Don't you want to be a nice big healthy girl with breasts like Yvonne here?"

That was my territory. I looked at Flynn up in front. *Do something.*

Flynn did. "Come on, Blowy. I dig your hostility but you got the wrong target."

Blowy corrected him: "A trivial target."

I had a flash like with Alden: something bad was going to happen, we were watching it happen, and there was nothing we could do. I felt temporarily relieved when we got to the Blot for pie.

It was near closing for the coffee shop. They were cleaning up. All the fluorescent lights were on and buzzing real loud. Blowy ordered pie. We all got coffee. I got pie too, for once. Maybe it would make me feel closer to Blowy. Patti Schmidt asked for a glass of water, no ice please. When it came with crushed ice she made a big production of taking out the ice with her spoon.

Maybe it was the grass, but the pies looked shiny and waxy

and unreal. I took a bite of mine to try to get that feeling to disappear. It half worked. Blowy examined the little canisters that came with the coffee.

"Non-dairy whitener," he announced. "An edible oil product. If something you're supposed to eat says edible on it you'd better not eat it."

Blowy was on one of those sharp, piercing, lucid highs. The grass had flip-flopped from withdrawn to aggressive. Flynn tried to calm him and tell him not to shoot for wrong targets. Unfortunately, everything on Kensington's main drag was a right target. A lucid high was the most antisocial high there was: it became perfectly and painfully clear that whatever happened to be nearby— in this case, the main drag of Kensington—was a false front, shiny and breakable like the lemon-cream pie frostings, in an urgent kind of a way.

Blowy stood up. "Welcome to the land of non-dairy whitener. Welcome to the land of edible oil products."

The calm in his voice announced a freak-out. Blowy headed for the door. We stood up.

"No, don't get up. I'm just going to practice a little pacification here on Main Street."

"Vinnie, do something!" Yvonne pleaded.

It was happening right before our eyes again. Flynn and I dug into our pockets for dollar bills and change to pay for the pies and coffees. By the time we got outside Blowy was a few hundred feet ahead of us.

He was standing in front of the sports shop. "Killing for sport," we heard him say very plainly from the other end of the block. "The toys must be kept away from the boys until the right moment. That's why this window is equipped with an alarm."

Then Blowy picked up one of those metal trash cans with the smile faces painted on them and bashed it against the window. The plate glass shattered like a bomb. An alarm started ringing.

Flynn and I ran for him. Blowy trotted down the street with the trash can held over his head. He addressed the Booke Nooke card shop.

"Well, if it's not the Bookie Nookie Card and Paper Shop." His voice was jovial, there was nothing crazy about it. "You've forgotten to take down your Mother's Day display—that was last

week. Or was it last month? Adieu, mother I never had—but I'll
tell you about that some other time.''

There was no alarm attached to the Booke Nooke window.
Nobody cared about the Hallmark cards. The glass caved in and
I could see Blowy's hands and face running with blood. Flynn
and I stopped running. We were close to him now.

''Blowy, Blowy,'' Flynn called softly, ''that's enough now,
man, please stop.''

''Just one more, okay?''

I saw the reflection of the red police flashers in the broken
glass and Blowy must have seen it too. He sprinted across the
street with the trash can. Those goddamned smile faces.

''Champ's Discount Food Outlet,'' he announced like a tour
guide. ''I hate those piles of day-old buns and factory-seconds
peas that the folks who don't make enough money have to buy.
It makes puffed-up girls who don't even put out.''

This time he let go of the trash can and it flew into Champ's
and a whole pyramid of mislabeled peas came crashing down
inside. He turned and faced us. There wasn't any craziness in
his face, just determination. It would have been better if there
had been.

''I have inner peace,'' he told us.

But not for long. The police arrived to try out their brand-new
Mace. It must have disturbed Blowy's lucidity. He collapsed on
the sidewalk; he was blinded and his throat was on fire. I felt
someone brush my hand and I pulled it away hard. Then I saw
it was Yvonne and I felt ashamed.

''We tried to stop him,'' I said to the cops.

''It's okay,'' a cop said.

''Look at this, just look at this waste.'' Flynn was crying.

The cops put Blowy in their car. They weren't hard on him at
all. That surprised me. They treated him like a child.

I LOOKED AT BLOWY through the bars. He didn't seem that bad.
His eyes were red and his skin was irritated, but his cuts were
all superficial.

"I'll only have to pay the deductible. The insurance will cover the rest. They'll charge me but they won't prosecute or anything."

"But?"

"I'll have to go see my Uncle."

We all knew it. There was really nothing much to say.

"I just got tired of waiting around. It's over."

The cops let us shake his hand through the bars.

Before we left the station I looked around for Chezevski. He wasn't there. Just a bunch of cops, talking on their radio, going about their business. They didn't even look at us.

Outside, Flynn held up the keys to Angel. "Blowy gave me these."

Great. Where do we go now?

I GOT ANOTHER VISIT from Chezevski, as promised. He was interested in Blowy, since Blowy was the only one who had broken the law in a public kind of a way. I figured Chezevski had two scenarios: either we killed Alden because he was doing head-trips and our vibrations got too different—whatever that meant. Or because of those vibrations, Alden got on a separate path, and in over his head with the wrong element. That was what we were inciting him to think.

It had not worked. Now that Blowy was off to some boot camp, Chezevski wanted to talk to me about him.

"Why do you think he did what he did—that vandalism?"

"He was all screwed up about the draft. He took the easy way out. He got some people to make up his mind for him."

Chezevski considered this like some kind of deep piece of evidence.

"Do you think what he did had something to do with the Alden boy's killing?"

"Alden wasn't trying to send him to Vietnam. Sure, the Alden thing was all part of the fucked-up atmosphere—"

"I agree."

I was shocked. A policeman had never agreed with me about anything before.

"But you can't make a simple equation out of it: Alden gets killed, Blowy runs away to the Army. It's not that simple."

"I see . . . Do you think the killing could be involved with drugs?"

"Drugs? I can't believe Alden was involved with people who would kill over drugs. I mean, a real heavy dealer might do that, but I don't see it."

"See what?"

"I don't see a real heavy dealer tramping around in the muddy old Hole with Chuck Alden."

"What do you think was behind his killing? The motive, I mean."

"I don't know . . . Power?"

"THAT'S YOUR FATHER'S PROBLEM," I summed it up for Yvonne. "He's got a crime and he doesn't know why. A motiveless crime. What do they say on the crime shows? Find out who the crime benefits. Well, this one doesn't benefit anybody. That's why it's unsolvable."

"But I want my daddy to solve it!"

"If you want him to, then I want him to too."

Any man would have given her anything she wanted. There was something so good and natural about Yvonne. I never knew a girl could want to do it as much as I did, and if by some chance I was slow on the uptake, she would remind me with a "Love, love," half-sung, half-said, and the way her voice was you knew she was talking about making love, not just calling me some pet name. I did not know where she got the use of those words. Maybe it was something women had that men didn't. I couldn't talk like that to her without hiding my face in her curtain of long red-brown hair.

In the middle of it Yvonne threw back the covers and pinched off one of my pubic hairs. My dick shriveled up.

"You sadist! What are you doing?"

"I'm gonna take this home to Daddy."

"Please stop saying Daddy when you're naked with me. It gives me the creeps."

"Daddy! Daddy! Daddy!"

"Watch out! I'm gonna make a citizen's arrest for unlawful fornication!"

"I'm gonna give this to him and save him a trip."

"Yeah? What for?" I got serious.

"Physical evidence."

"What's that mean?"

"I don't know. I'm only telling you what I happen to overhear. *Doličný materiál*—physical evidence. I also know that oral and rectal swabs showed no traces of seminal fluid, and that there were no drugs or significant alcohol content in his blood."

"Jesus Christ!" I imagined Alden stretched out on a table while some guys in rubber gloves stuck Q-tips down his throat and up his ass. It was like talking about taking a crap at the dinner table. Death in its indecency and us all naked and splendid.

"Do you want to know about this stuff or don't you?"

"Sure, sure. Keep me posted. Maybe he'd like one from you."

"He'd ask a matron in that case."

"I'll save her a trip. Let me see, here's a few right here . . . but they're too pretty to pick, like wildflowers. So soft to the touch."

"So sweet to the tongue," she suggested. "If it's all right with you."

Why wouldn't it be?

FLYNN DID NOT LOOK entirely comfortable at the controls of Blowy's Angel. Flynn did not have Blowy's long legs, and the driver's seat was too far back. But the mechanism that slid it forward had corroded into place several model-years ago.

I did not feel entirely comfortable in Blowy's car either, with that long empty space behind us.

It was two weeks since Blowy had committed his public mischief. He was with his Uncle now. We had not heard anything from him yet.

"So we're all that's left of the Kensington Krazies," Flynn said.

I turned around. It was a long way back to the tailgate.

"We got Yvonne," I said.

"She's your girl."

"That's not my fault. We still got Patti Schmidt and Lo. We got Stotl."

"Carl the Deep," Flynn called him.

"And there's you and me."

"We're a great pair," Flynn said pessimistically. "Elephant Ears and Flynn the Loveless. You had Alden and I had Blowy, things were equal then. Then you lost Alden and I lost Blowy—all right. But then you got Yvonne."

A weird way of looking at things. Flynn's way.

"We could say we have each other," I suggested. "That's what people tell each other after they've lost everything else."

"We could say that," he admitted, begrudging, "but it won't be the same."

"Nobody said it was going to be the same. Anyway, summer's here. When fall comes we'll all go our separate ways anyway. Something might happen in the meantime."

"It probably will, the rate things are going now."

We drove down Gilbert Avenue. Then past Shawmut. Then the main drag. Flynn was taking us on a tour of all the places we had been with Blowy.

"You know, the cop is going to come and clip our pubes," said Flynn.

"So I understand."

"Patti's too."

"Patti's pubes—that's a horrible thought. Where did you hear that?"

"My parents." Flynn looked uncomfortable, like anyone does when they admit to being privileged. "They're going to spring for a lawyer for me. I think Patti's parents are going to do the same thing."

"A lawyer? What for? We're not on trial."

"I know, I know. But that's what my parents want. They say I should be protected. Counseled . . . You know, we don't have to let him clip our pubes if we don't want to."

"No?"

"Not right off, anyway," Flynn qualified. "If he wants to do it and we don't want him to, he can't until he gets a subpoena from a grand jury."

"My pubic hair subpoenaed by a grand jury! What an honor! Hear that, boys?" I gave myself a scratch.

"And then, every time he comes and talks to us, we don't have to talk to him if we don't want to, and if we do, we can have a lawyer there."

"Is that what you're doing?" I asked Flynn.

"Not me, my parents. They don't want me to talk to the cop."

"Yeah? Why not?"

"I don't know . . . because he's a cop. Because if you have anything to do with the cops it's a shame to your name. You're *involved.*"

"I think I know why I've gotten so many visits from the cop," I told Flynn. "I'm talking to him."

He took it as an accusation. I suppose it was. "Yeah, well, it's true. After I talked to him the first time, my parents got me this lawyer. He told me today that I'd already said everything I knew, and that there wasn't any use saying the same thing over and over again."

"So that's the loco parentis thing! Shit, Flynn, your lawyer's had some kind of effect."

Chezevski had tried to slip around the parental blockade and get to us at school. The assistant principal stopped him at the door—how he knew Chezevski was on his way was a mystery. The same way Flynn's lawyer knew the cops' next move, I guess. On orders from the principal, who was hiding somewhere behind his secretary, Chezevski was shown the door on grounds of loco parentis. The school acted in the place of the parents when the children were there. If the parents did not wish their children to speak to the police at home, the assistant principal said, we cannot allow them to speak to them here, in our school, since that is against the parents' wishes.

Meanwhile, the remnants of the Kensington Krazies were hiding behind the pillars of authority we had so recently wanted to tear down.

"Are you gonna let him do it? Clip them?" Flynn came back to the question. It was weird to see how he had changed. Contact with his new lawyer had drained all the craziness out of him. He had gotten all tentative. It had to do with having a privilege I didn't have.

"I guess so." I had not considered the alternative. "I've co-operated with him so far—in my fashion."

Flynn barked a dry, nervous laugh. I had to laugh too. I ended up looking like Mr. Policeman's best friend because I was willing to feed him a string of half-truths. I had no other choice, not with Yvonne.

"The lawyer says Chezevski must be wanting to compare our hair with the hair he found on Alden's body. There's other things too, like the burned stuff in the clearing."

"That belongs to Mayo," I reminded Flynn. "But the hair stuff gives me the creeps. I mean, picture some of your hair being buried alive with Alden."

We drove for a while and thought about our hairs, which stood for our involvement.

"It's funny," I said to Flynn, "it's like the authorities, except for the cops, don't really want this thing solved. They want to look the other way. Okay, maybe you're not cooperating, maybe you have a lawyer. But nobody's cooperating. The whole town is looking the other way."

"Poor Chezevski."

That was the first Krazy thing Flynn had said. Finally he was back on track! Poor Chezevski, digging around in Kensington's Konscience, looking for the stain. Poor Chezevski, rattling around all alone down there in that big, empty cavern.

Flynn swung the wheel. "That brings me to the subject of the Hole. I hear they want to raze it."

"They want to raise it? Like up to ground level?"

"No, they want to raze it. They want to tear down the Hole."

It was a pleasure being Krazy with Flynn again. Krazy meant accurate. When the city council wants to tear down a hole, you have to be Krazy.

"If it's a Hole," I reasoned, "they don't want to tear it down, they want to tear it up. What they really want to do, Bobby Flynn, is to fill it up."

"Fill it in. Fill, fill, fill, they'll never fill it to the brim."

"A hungry Hole. A void. How many voids can fit in infinity?"

"Stop, stop." Flynn took his hands off the wheel and clapped them over his ears.

The city council really did want to fill in the Hole. That wasn't some Krazy invention. They had a big meeting, it was in all the papers. The problem was that the Hole belonged to no one. And no one wanted to claim it. The chief of police got up and proposed that the land be turned into a park. He testified that the place had been a thorn in his blue side for the past twenty-five years. But the parks commissioner would have none of that. He declared that his commission was not in the business of law enforcement, that the Hole was a police department problem, and that no one would want to spend his free time in a half-drained swamp anyway, and that the purpose of a park was to serve the immediate citizenry and there was hardly any of that around, which is why the Hole was the Hole in the first place. Then the commissioner nailed home the coffin door. Converting the Hole into a respectable park would cost half a million dollars, which meant passing a bond issue. Of course none of the city councillors got up and said it out loud, but they were not about to call a bond issue on turning the Hole into a park. That would be like asking the citizens to vote on the best way to forget that the whole Alden business had happened in the first place.

Then the mayor was struck by a brilliant idea. Hand the whole Hole over to the developers. Let them build colonial-style houses on top of it.

A COUPLE DAYS LATER two things happened because of Chuck Alden. Sgt.-Det. Chezevski came calling with his evidence bag. And the Hole was not razed—it was bulldozed.

"You can start whenever you want to," I told Chezevski, showing him a chair, "I don't have any lawyer looking after me."

He got down to business. He took out his little regulation-issue sterilized scissors and snipped off a hair from my head.

"Unbutton your shirt, please."

He went for an armpit and a chest hair. Nothing to it.

"I'm going to have to ask you to open your trousers."

He rummaged around and found the right hair and snipped it. If he only knew his daughter had laid her sweet head there a couple nights ago—but in his way he did know, I reminded myself.

"Take off your shoe."

He took my foot measure with one of those sliding metal scales they use in shoestores. Then he moved to the kitchen table.

"You've cooperated with me, and I know you know it. So I'm going to let you into my confidence. We found some burned clothing and shoes in the Hole near where the Alden boy was murdered.''

He waited for me to react but there was nothing to react to yet. I was making sure not to be too helpful.

"There was a T-shirt with a Kensington High crest on it."

"It couldn't have belonged to one of us," I said automatically. He jumped on it. "Oh, no? Why not?"

"Because none of us would wear the symbol of authority."

"Not even Charles Alden?"

"Especially not Charles Alden."

Chezevski thought about it for a minute.

"But you used to wear the crest," he countered, "you used to be on the cross-country team."

"That was an athletic uniform, not a T-shirt," I corrected him with some pride. "Anyway, they threw us off the team a while ago."

"What did you do?"

"We committed a desecration. We took our Magic Markers and drew little pipes with smoke coming out of them in the Kensington lion's mouth on our shorts. We got kicked off for that. And the team hasn't gone anywhere since."

"What kind of person would wear a Kensington T-shirt, if it wasn't your kind?"

That was the question I wanted. "A straight, a rah-rah type. An upstanding member of the community!"

Chezevski digested the information. "We're not getting too far with them. The kids follow the example of their elders. If they see the principal of their school trying to evade the truth and being successful about it, what does that teach them?"

Keep talking, I thought, and we'll consider you for membership in the Kensington Krazies. But then he got straight again.

"I hear a lot about vibrations from you young people. What are vibrations, anyway?"

I swallowed my laughter. Chezevski was plain absurd as a policeman. Which made his question a good one.

"I don't know, it's just something we say . . . It's a kind of superstition people have: when things are going good or not good with someone or something, they talk about vibrations. In a way it doesn't mean anything at all."

Chezevski did not like my answer. But I couldn't do any better: no one really knew what the word "vibrations" meant. It was a password that got you through doors through which Chezevski could not pass.

Later that day Stotl called up. If he hadn't we would have missed a major event in Kensington's natural history.

"The Hole is full of bulldozers," he shouted into the phone, "we'd better go out and take a look."

He had gotten over his resentment at being used to discover Alden's body. Now he just wanted to be where the action was.

I called up Flynn and we got all the Krazy remnants together. A bunch of job ends and factory seconds. Me, Flynn, Stotl, Patti Schmidt and Yvonne. It was going to be a sentimental journey.

We pulled off Gilbert Avenue and watched. Two yellow bulldozers were going back and forth over the Hole, just like they were mowing a lawn, knocking down everything they could. The brush, the saplings. They were smoothing out the heaps of whatever there was down there. By order of city council, until they could find some developers adventurous enough to want to fill the whole swamp and stick colonials on top of it. The city had to do something about the Hole: it was a social problem in a time of social problems. Leveling it was an intermediate solution. A form of looking the other way.

"The Hole, R.I.P. Born when this country was, died when the sixties did." I shielded my eyes as the dust drifted over our way. It was my mourning imagination, no doubt, but I swore I saw a couple of young elms with psychedelic designs on the trunks fall to the bulldozers' blades.

"The Hole lives," Flynn said.

"The Hole is," said Stotl.

"We'll find another Hole," Yvonne promised.

"The Hole is everywhere," Patti Schmidt said in her vague way.

Charles Alden did not say anything. Neither did Blowy Bloedell. They missed their turns.

We were getting to be experts in funeral orations, considering our tender age. First Charles Alden. Then a vacant lot.

"THAT WAS SOMETHING," I said to Yvonne, "they destroyed the scene of the crime. Right before our eyes."

"They can never do anything with that land. If they build houses, the houses will be haunted."

I had found a new bed for Yvonne and me, one that could be used in those sweet, hazy summer evening hours before the yards of Kensington grew dark and sheltering. For two years I had janitored at the Kensington city hall, a job I was not going to get again this summer. My last act was to take a copy of the keys to the place. On the top floor of the turn-of-the-century building was an American Legion hall for World War One veterans, a real museum with old-fashioned pool tables, regimental flags and long, smooth leather couches with spittoons at either end.

We were naked on a leather couch, very close together, in our juices. It was hot outside now. A pink heat haze shimmered over Kensington to the west. Yvonne and I were alone in 1917. There were no more World War One legionnaires, old geezers with their flies undone who would tell you that in the winter of nineteen-whatever, it was so cold they had to piss on the radiators to unfreeze their cars. The ones who were left could not climb the long, winding flight of stairs to their club anymore.

Me on Yvonne, Yvonne on me. Afterward we got up to admire the view from the tall windows. Her naked feet in the dust on the floor. The wet spot on the shiny smooth couch.

"Don't wipe it off. Leave it—we're part of history that way."

She had more imagination than me in those kinds of things. Girls always do. I was too timid about sex. Too amazed she would want to do it with me.

"Before school let out," Yvonne said, "I did some work for extra credit. I got my hands on this."

She opened her little Indian cotton purse, which was hanging on one of the stand-up ashtrays. She gave me a piece of paper. It was one of those slippery, chemical-smelling copies you could make at school.

I read:

The Group decided to execute the Victim on grounds of weakness. His weakness was spreading and endangered even the Leader with contamination. Since these executions were not yet legal, the Group had to find a safe place where its rites would be undisturbed. In the woods, at night, there was a different world so near, yet so far from civilization. The Victim was surrounded, a chant went up. Every time he tried to escape he was met with another fist. We closed around him. At first he thought it was a game, like the other ones he had played. But then he saw the evil in the Leader's eyes . . .

"What is this thing? Where'd you get this? Does this belong to—"

"You guessed it! From the pen of Tom Mayo."

"It's ripped off from *Lord of the Flies*!"

"That's why you get As in English." Yvonne laughed. "They were studying that book earlier this year."

"In Fundies?" Fundamental English was the track for slow learners.

Yvonne nodded.

"They should keep this stuff out of the wrong hands!"

"For a Fundies student, he doesn't write that bad," Yvonne pointed out.

I read a little bit more. I didn't agree with her. The paper was the worst mishmash of Spiderman, Sgt. Rock and bad-trip acid-rock lyrics. All those capital letters on Leader and Victim, those secret handshakes and mysterious powers, all mixed in with words to acid-rock songs that nobody ever understood in the first place. But it was a faultless description of Mayo and Alden. The contamination, the head-tripping. And Mayo described the Hole down to the last tuft of bushes. It was like a treasure map to the sickness.

As I read it, I thought that when Mayo finally did the real thing, it must have been a comedown after all that fantasizing. I sensed glimmers of weakness in him, something rotten and unstable. Fear of contamination by Alden. I began to see we might be able to do something with that.

"Can I ask you where you got this?" I held up the paper.

"That's just a copy. The original is in a safe place."

"You stole it from him," I concluded.

"I got it out of his books when he wasn't looking."

She was proud of herself. And I was proud of her too. "You forgot to check the date," she said.

It was hard to make out through the grimy copy. Mayo had written the paper a good month before Alden was killed.

"He planned the whole goddamned thing!" I nearly shouted. "That's really sick! He was plotting it! He rehearsed it!"

Yvonne nodded her head. "I don't know which way is worse."

It was a combination of so many things. The rip-off of *Lord of the Flies*, the naive comic-book stuff, the sickness of premeditated murder. Sick craziness and banality all mixed up together.

"The worst part is that it's probably useless as any kind of evidence," Yvonne said.

"But look at it! It's practically a confession."

Yvonne shook her head sadly. "I'm a policeman's daughter. This is the kind of thing that policemen are always complaining about getting thrown out of court. But I think we still have a chance. It has to do with this." I had to ward off her attack on my short and curlies. "Detective Yvonne's been doing some snooping on the case. Your hair was found on Chuck's body—your head hair, thank goodness, or I'd drop you. And Patti Schmidt's, uh, maiden hair was also found, entwined in poor Chuck's pubes. Isn't that romantic?"

"Cut the crap, would you?" I was already in the witness box. "That just means we were, like, close. It doesn't mean we killed him! I mean, what about Patti Schmidt's maidens?"

"That's exactly what I'm trying to say. For a civilian you're not bad. We all had what you might call familiarity with Chuck. Hair travels easily and clings. But there was one set of hairs not accounted for that didn't come from any of us."

"That could have come from Mayo!"

"That's what I'm hoping for. It could have come from me or Blowy. But let's say it belongs to Mayo. I send this incriminating document anonymously, there's a spare set of hairs, they turn out to be Mayo's—then maybe something will happen!"

The club for old men who had fought in the good war was dark except for the glow of Yvonne's naked knees tucked under her chin. Outside, the tree-stunting mercury-vapor lamps were buzzing. The sky was black overhead and there was a rosy-blue line to the west. There were tiny moments like this one when we both felt really free. I wondered why there were some girls like Patti Schmidt and Lo who hated their bodies and made it impossible for anyone who wanted to love them, and then there was someone like Yvonne.

YVONNE CALLED ME two days later.
   "I can't talk now. My daddy's got the letter. He's gonna use it somehow. I love you."
   Then the click and the dial tone.

THE NATURAL HISTORY of Tom Mayo, as overheard in Czech and leaked through the privilege of Bobby Flynn's lawyer. The Kensington police system, I discovered, was full of informers, and not the kind you would have expected, or suspected.
   Chezevski decided to drop in unannounced at Mayo's place on Ashland Avenue. It was one of those newish apartment blocks along the railroad tracks, new and getting old fast, with cracks springing in the oatmeal walls and the sashes not closing tight from the one-hundred-car freights going by so near and hard. Tangles of baby bikes with training wheels and empty diaper boxes waiting to go down to the trash.
   Chezevski wanted to catch Mayo by surprise, uncoached, before the whole parent-lawyer censorship machine could get set and freeze the truth. Mayo opened the door; Chezevski identified himself and stepped inside. It was not a search, not an arrest. It was a little conversation. A hunch.
   Chezevski started in. "I saw that essay you wrote for your English class. You've got a real gift."
   Fear ran through Mayo's body like lightning. Chezevski liked what he saw.
   "Do you always describe murders before they happen?"
   "I don't know what you're talking about." Mayo's voice was flat and dead-sounding.
   "Let me refresh your memory." Chezevski could feel Mayo's nervousness about to bloom into something interesting. He could practically taste the words on the kid's tongue.
   "You wrote a little essay for your English class about how

some kids ganged up to kill another kid. Then all of a sudden the Alden boy gets killed, in a way awfully similar to the way you describe it, in a place awfully similar to the Hole. Be honest, Tom. When was the last time you saw the Alden boy alive? Where were you the Saturday night he was killed? Did you ever hit Charles Alden, with your fist or anything else? With a piece of concrete?''

Then a bedroom door opened and a woman walked into the living room. She was pretty but used-looking, dressed in her best, like she was planning to go out for the evening, even though it wasn't five yet. Let it be his sister, Chezevski prayed, or the cleaning lady. His prayers went unanswered. It was Lynda Mayo, Tom's mother. Just the kind of counterauthority Chezevski did not want around.

She came up behind her son and even before she asked Chezevski who he was, she put her hand on Tom's shoulder and gave him a little squeeze. There was something sexual to it, something to toughen him up. That was the end of the interview. The end of the truth. Mayo flipped back into control. His eyes got clear, he began to rock back and forth on his heels. The rest of the conversation was the usual useless, routine ballet. Lynda Mayo asked Chezevski if he were the police, as if he had come to read the water meter. She knew exactly what her rights were. Chezevski wondered if she had ever been up on a soliciting charge.

Like Bobby Flynn, Mayo was a noncooperator. Chezevski had to go through the subpoena business to get a set of hairs to compare to the unaccounted ones on Alden's body. When he returned to Mayo's apartment with his evidence bag, he found that little hard-ass Mayo, who had called him ''copper'' to his face like Edward G. Robinson, had equipped himself with Harry Bartlesby, a downtown lawyer who could find his way blindfolded through the halls of the Cook County Court Building right to the chambers of a friendly judge. People who live in places with oatmeal walls can't usually afford this kind of defense, Chezevski reflected as he took out his sterile evidence scissors. Bartlesby watched in hopes of a technicality.

''You might want to leave the room,'' Chezevski suggested to Lynda Mayo when it came time for the pubic sample.

She declined the invitation. Chezevski chose hairs close to the organ, and applied a malicious little twist before dropping them into the bag. There was no chest hair to speak of. Chezevski found one in the armpit.

The ceremony was over. That was Mayo's cue to speak.

"I've been thinking about what you asked me the other day," he said.

Chezevski looked at Bartlesby, but Bartlesby was looking at Lynda Mayo's ass. His way of appearing unconcerned.

"I was in the Hole the night Alden got killed."

"Did you see or hear anything out of the ordinary?"

"I heard some scuffling noises, you know, voices and stuff, but it didn't last long."

"Did you go and see what it was?"

"No."

"Why not?"

"In the Hole you're better off not sticking your nose into other people's business."

"Even a big guy like you who can take care of himself?"

"Hey, I can't take on everybody."

"Were you alone in the Hole?"

"Yeah."

"Is that a place you go alone to?"

"You can. You can meet people there."

"Even if you're better off not sticking your nose into other people's business?" Chezevski paused to make it sound like Mayo had contradicted himself. "Did you see anybody down there?"

"No. That's how come I came back."

"Back where?"

"Back here, to the house. There wasn't anybody I knew in the Hole, or at least I didn't see them, so I came back."

"What time was it?"

"I don't know, around ten o'clock. I don't own a watch."

"It was ten o'clock." Lynda Mayo supplied the alibi. "I was watching television. The news had just come on."

The autopsy showed Alden had died between ten-thirty and two in the morning. Mayo had given himself just enough margin. The sure signs of being coached.

"Did you know Charles Alden?"

"I knew him to see him."

"What do you think of him?"

Mayo shrugged. "He was a hippie. A sissy."

End of conversation. Bartlesby had not opened his mouth once. The man's silence was truly golden.

I HAD NO JOB for the summer until the singing aunts and uncles came to eat the three-bean salad and drink lemonade one hot Sunday afternoon. One of the uncles worked for the Jewish Welfare League, an agency that found jobs for out-of-work Jews. My father had been one of his clients, in unhappier times. "What is family for?" my uncle would say whenever his assistance was mentioned, always as an embarrassment. Our embarrassment at having needed help made him embarrassed, which only made him want to help us more.

"What do you want to do?" he asked me.

"Something dirty and well-paying," I told him.

"You can forget about shoes," the socialist-shoe-salesman uncle said. "It's dirty, what with all those socks, but it pays like shit."

"Really, you don't have to help us," my father said. "He'll find something."

My welfare uncle waved him off. "What have you done before?"

"Janitor." I blushed.

"There's no shame, no shame. Why don't you do it again?"

"I'm not getting hired back."

"Anti-Semitism," the socialist uncle said confidently. Everyone agreed. Impossible that maybe I was not such a great janitor.

"Maybe I have something for you," said the Jewish-welfare uncle. "It's good and dirty. And you won't be put out for anti-Semitism because it is a Jewish-owned business."

What other kind of business would it have been?

The next week I was out in the wide world of work, without a Kensington Krazy anywhere to be seen. I was just as glad. We were finding it harder to get together, and harder to stay together once we were there. Flynn and I hurtled at each other and missed; when we hit it was painful. Patti and Lo were spectators, and when they tired of not being on center stage, like children they would commit an attention-getting act. Stotl was a clown with a hard-on. Blowy was Flynn's invisible playmate: he had great bearing on the proceedings, but like the Viet Cong, you could never engage him directly. Meanwhile, with his head like a rotton vegetable and one gym shoe sticking out of the soft dirt, Chuck Alden watched and grinned.

It was only a matter of time before Yvonne and I were tainted.

I wasn't sorry to be a member of the Beef Boners and Sausage Workmen of America, Local 100, serving the Star of Zion packinghouse. The Jewish-welfare uncle was right: dirty and well-paying. I took as much of both those ingredients as any man could stand. Overtime was at a precious time-and-a-half, and some days I was at Star of Zion for ten or twelve hours.

I started at seven in the morning, running wieners through an unpacking machine. They made the hot dogs in this inedible plastic casing that had to be taken off after the dogs had been cooked. The machine had a razor blade adjusted just right to split the casing open without touching the meat. Then a blast of steam would blow the casing away and the hot dog would emerge out the other end of the machine, all shiny and whole and full of kosher splendor. After which a team of three-hundred-pound Polish ladies would pack the dogs. The ladies talked and giggled and elbowed each other in the ribs all day, going on about how much they fucked with their papas after they came back from eight hours of packing nitrate-pink sausages.

My machine was invented by a lunatic. The razor blade had to be replaced five times a day. It was always maladjusting itself and cutting too deep. The hot dog would burst when it came through the steam, resulting in a great explosion of kosher meat. I had to dismantle the machine to clean it, scalding my face and hands with the steam.

As the day went on I moved closer to the essence of meat. I Cryovacked tongues, which consisted of slipping a pickled or boiled beef tongue into a plastic sack and sucking out all the air with the Cryovacking machine to make a perfect vacuum, which is something like the void, or satori: very hard to achieve.

Lunch hour was also a journey toward the essence of meat, though of a different kind. We walked to the tavern for lunch through the Water Market, secure with our razor-sharp four-inch knives dangling from the straps of our steel-toed boots. In between trailers backed up to the docks, often a commercial transaction would be taking place. Once a woman was taking it from behind from a truck driver, standing up, doggy-style. I stopped to watch. I had never seen it being done in the open before, in broad daylight.

The woman looked up from her labor. "So I'm getting fucked. So what's it to you?"

Red Watson, my foreman, tugged on my sleeve. "She's got a point, kid."

Before lunch we went fishing in the vat. I took a long stainless-steel trident and harpooned one of the tongues peacefully boiling away in the greasy, spiced water, like a giant whale in the ocean. Fishing was a two-man expedition. Red Watson would harpoon the beast and hold it up, dripping, in the air in front of me. With my knife I would slice enough off for sandwiches for both of us. With the rolls we brought from home and the mustard supplied by the tavern, we had lunch every day courtesy of Star of Zion.

I had never seen drinking like that. Red was moderate: a shot and a beer, maybe two. He was a foreman. There were not too many blacks with that title, and he was not about to slip up. But the rest of the factory ran on alcohol. Besides what they had for lunch, almost everyone had a half-pint of bourbon under his smock. Even the DPs drank. Before that I never knew Jews could drink whiskey. They had been town butchers somewhere in Poland before the Nazis got to them. The Star of Zion recruited them out of the DP camps after the war to come to Chicago and carve up cows in the Water Market. Because I was new, they figured I hadn't heard all their stories before, jokes about waiting for the Messiah, things like that.

The Water Market was another world. I wished the Kensington Krazies could come down and see it. If an open pickup truck took a corner too fast and a grapefruit flew off the top, half-rupturing on the street, there was always a gang of men ready to pounce on it. At night, when we dumped the trash, old ladies would be waiting in the alley to pick through the garbage for scraps of meat off the bone and exploded hot-dog bits. And there were always a few hippie photography students hanging around when we were unloading the carcasses from the slaughterhouse.

"This is real life," I shouted to them, "take it in black and white!"

IN MID-SUMMER FLYNN called. "Let's go row. Yogi wants to talk to Boo-Boo."

That meant he wanted to talk to me. Ever since Blowy left, Flynn had turned strange. He had warned me that day in the car: he had no one for himself and now he was drifting. He began referring to us as cartoon characters. He had really absorbed his American culture. Sometimes he was Fred Flintstone and I was Barney Rubble. Yvonne was Wilma. Or else it was Yogi and Boo-Boo. A cooler of beer was a pik-a-nik basket.

Stranger than the average bear.

Lo was back in circulation. She and Patti Schmidt, Stotl and Flynn and Yvonne and I all loaded into Angel. We drove past the defoliated Hole and out to Long John Slough, where we could rent rowboats and see some nature.

At the wheel, Flynn declared a moment of silence. We rolled southbound on Gilbert Avenue. No one thought to ask whom the moment was for. When it was up, Flynn burst into song, in loud dirge time:

> I'm no fool, no sirree,
> I'm copping out 'fore I'm twenty-three—
> And always put your conscience in a bind!

In the backseat, Patti Schmidt let out a sob, sharp and pointy like the ribs in her chest. Stotl took her hand. Lo took the other and began actively consoling her. Lo was like one of those patients in the loony bin whose way of being crazy is playing nurse.

"That moment of silence wasn't for *him*," Flynn said spitefully.

At Long John Slough we turned our pockets inside out and came up with enough money for two rowboats.

"Boo-Boo's gonna ride with Yogi," Flynn told the others.

I don't think they knew what he was talking about. That was the idea, I suppose.

We launched into the slimy water, all green and thick under the surface with algae, like some kind of soup that had gone bad. The slough was part of the great Kensington swamp system that had given us the late Hole. There was just enough draft to clear a rowboat like ours. In the middle of the swampy lake a hump of land formed an island. To get there you had to row through a forest of bare poles that had once been trees. Woodpeckers and carpenter ants had hollowed them out and stripped the bark, and all the branches had long since fallen off. A forest of tree trunks standing knee-deep in the slimy water. It was prehistoric. A Krazy view of nature: everything bare and against itself.

With Flynn rowing we moved swiftly ahead of the others. He launched right in.

"Remember when you led everyone off to watch Alden get it? You had them all crouch in the bushes instead of laying back on the hood and letting things take their proper course. And when you came back everyone promised not to do anything without telling everyone else first. I never went on that treasure hunt, and not because I didn't want to get *involved*—I always thought the treasure was worthless. Fool's gold. Illusion of the poets. But I ended up involved anyway, and that's okay, I was part of the evening. But you know I didn't like what it did to Blowy. Maybe we couldn't have saved him, I don't know. But I'm willing to bet he'd still be here if it weren't for that.

"And now my leaky lawyer tells me Mr. Policeman received a purloined paper written by the unaccused. Don't ask me where my leaky lawyer gets this kind of thing. An ear to the ground in the cemetery, maybe. That's what he gets paid for, getting his ears dirty. Would you know anything about this, by any chance?"

"Sure I would. Yvonne ripped a paper off Mayo, don't ask me how. It was an essay he wrote for Fundies class, some kind of copy of *Lord of the Flies*. It talked all about the murder—written a month before it happened. A real coincidence."

"You're all excited about it, aren't you two?"

"She sent it to the police—anonymously. *Then* she told me about it."

"I see. Now we're trying to get the unaccused accused. I thought the name of the game was silence."

The boat drifted into the grove of dead trees. It nosed into the trunks. There was a hollow sound.

"That's what I thought too," I admitted.

"Then call her off! Tell her to stop—unless you're in on it."

"If I told her to stop she'd knee my nuts."

"She certainly has enough opportunity."

"Get off it, Flynn, goddamnit! You want to talk about the case or you want to play Flynn the Loveless? My line hasn't changed. Only Yvonne . . . she has this thing: she wants to put her father onto Mayo but without making it sound like it came from us."

"Sounds absurd," Flynn declared.

"It does, actually. Absurd. But not impossible."

"So now the name of the game is a very noisy silence, like the one inside my head. I just don't want to be caught toeing the hard party line while everyone else is playing footsy with the cops."

We steered through the trees. You could see the ants running over the wood, busy tearing down what was left. There was a little stretch of open water, then the island. I took the oars. Flynn leaned back and watched me row.

"Just keep me posted if you send any more anonymous letters," he said, mock cheerful. "I just don't like hearing what my friends are doing through my lawyer."

I beached the boat on a sandy spot. Flynn unloaded the Styrofoam cooler. We watched the second boat come in with Stotl and the three girls. He had one oar, Lo had the other. They were moving mostly in circles. It looked like they were having a better time than Flynn and I had had. Finally their boat came floating in sideways and crashed into the island. Stotl pulled it onto dry land. Lo was working at an old-people's home and when she stepped by me I got a whiff off her like old piss. Strangely, I felt my dick want to stand up.

We pitched our camp around the cooler. Stotl took off his shirt. I was hot from rowing and I did the same, though there was no breeze to cool off my skin.

"If you guys can do that, I can too."

It was Patti Schmidt. She unbuttoned her light-blue Sears work shirt. It fell around her waist where it was tucked in.

"Jesus Christ!" Stotl swore. He scrambled into his shirt.

Bravely, I contemplated Patti's torso. She looked like the pictures of the Auschwitz survivors my parents had at home. Her ribs were like a washboard and her skin was flaking away in patches.

She looked at me looking at her. She had a weird, half-proud smile. "That's lanugo," she told me like she was some kind of tour guide.

"What are you talking about?"

She ran her hands over her forearms. There was downy white hair growing there. She had studied her disease thoroughly, not to overcome it but to glory in it. Congratulations, you win round one, you out-crazied us all by a mile.

Yvonne was the first one to come up with something to say. "Don't sit in the sun, Patti, you'll get burned."

For once she did as she was told. When she thought no one was looking, she wriggled back into her shirt again.

Flynn cleared his throat ceremoniously.

"Well, now, before we open the pik-a-nik basket, I'd like to spring a surprise on you all. I'm not referring to some kind of drug, we've had enough of them already. I'm talking about a letter from Blowy."

"Far out," Stotl intoned, "our very own Army man."

"Our scout, our runner-ahead, our weather forecaster," Flynn added. "It's a week old, like the hot-dog buns down at Champ's Discount Food Outlet. But we haven't been together for a week. The working life, you know."

Then he shut up and read:

I've said it before and I'll say it again: the Army is a hipper place than I imagined. A certain amount of weed makes the rounds here, the kind of weed I introed you to under the barge bridge, parachuted in by who knows, the Viet Congs maybe, to pervert our morale. I don't hate the Viet Congs yet and I don't know anyone who does. We're all in suspense here, actually, waiting to go over and shoot real people and get shot at in return. There's major silence on that point here in camp. The brass does a Zen trip on us (though they wouldn't call it that): when you get there you'll understand, and you can't understand till you get there.

I feel far from CA here. I'm sure you think that's why I went. Far, maybe, but not far enough. Sure, sure, we all feel like we did him in because we let him go and do his own thing... Anyway, don't ask me why I went: I went because I thought it could never happen to me.

I tried launching the Jiminy Crickets song here but it went over like a lead you-know-what. Everyone is like real intensely into staying alive, if not living, and Jiminy is forever chirping on about the unmentionable.

Well, they say travel broadens the mind so I'm off to the land of the Yellow Man real soon. Who would have thought that a Kensington Krazy landscape artist would have ended up in a scrape like this? Oh, well. There it is. Be good to Angel.

A letter from the other side.

"He might already be over there. I bet he is. When I read it I was blown away. I'm still blown away," Flynn said.

"What would Blowy want us to do?" Yvonne wondered.

"I don't think we can know."

"If we can't know," Flynn reasoned, "the best thing is for us bears to drink some beers. I declare open season on pik-a-nik baskets."

I pulled the cans of Drewry's off the white plastic six-pack straps and handed them around. Everybody was eager to get a little beer in their bellies.

Flynn raised his aluminum can. "May Blowy come back in one piece and reclaim his automobile."

"I drink to that. And to 2-s deferments for those with a stomach to play the game—like me. I got my admission notice to a big-time university yesterday. I won't have to spend the rest of my natural life chopping up kosher cows at Star of Zion."

We drank. We drank to not having to know the pressure Blowy was under now. I drank to Yvonne's getting into art school at a university two car-hours away, and to my purchase of my father's Dodge Coronet 500 with the slant-6 engine. Yvonne drank to the Sgt.-Det.'s cracking the Mayo nut. We fell into one of those noisy silences Flynn talked about. The sound of people drinking to different things.

THE NATURAL HISTORY of Tom Mayo, part two. The last information Bobby Flynn would leak to me through his leaky lawyer.

Joliet. The state crime lab looked down its nose into its microscope and concluded that this new set of hairs, freshly arrived in shiny new evidence pouches, possessed the same width and texture as the previously unidentified hairs found on Alden's body.

Chezevski visited the Mayo household. Lynda Mayo opened

the door. She looked as though she were expecting company, his or someone else's.

She click-clicked across the living room, displaying her well-made thirty-six-year-old buttocks. Then she turned and stopped in front of a closed door that Chezevski took to be her son Tom's.

"I'm afraid I've been instructed not to allow you to talk to Tom unless the lawyer is here. And lawyers are so expensive we might as well pay attention to what they say, don't you think?"

As if you were actually picking up the tab, Chezevski thought to himself.

"Would you care for something to eat or drink?"

"What the fuck's the matter with you people?" he said in Czech.

"Pardon me?"

As he expected, Lynda Mayo did not understand Czech. Taking silence for refusal, she disappeared into the kichen, where the telephone was, closing the plastic accordion partition behind her.

As if by magic, ten minutes later a car door slammed outside with that solid Cadillac sound. The awkward flapping of a downtown lawyer's briefcase against a suited thigh coming down the hallway, sidestepping the diaper boxes. Bartlesby rang the door bell and opened the door simultaneously.

Lynda Mayo fetched her boy from his room. He came out blinking and looking foolish, as if he'd just gotten through jerking off.

Chezevski addressed Bartlesby. "The lab shows that hairs found on the victim's body are a perfect match for the ones on your client's head."

Bartlesby nodded, as though he had been expecting it all along.

"What that tells us is that your client had close physical contact with the victim immediately before he was buried—alive, Mr. Bartlesby, buried alive. Your client's hair was also found on some half-burned clothing, a Kensington High T-shirt that he probably burned himself to get rid of incriminating evidence."

"That's your interpretation of a shred of physical evidence. As you know, physical evidence in itself is insufficient to convict."

"I thought your client might have something to say."

"Is he under arrest?"

"I don't know. Did you hear me place him under arrest?"

"Detective, I find this—"

"I find this whole case pretty sickening too!"

Bartlesby switched into smooth. "Please believe me, I understand your feelings."

"You don't understand the surface, Bartlesby. Now what does your client have to say about it?"

"Tom, do you have anything to say? Remember, you don't have to speak if you don't want to. It's your right."

Mayo snapped to attention. He took the cue. Chezevski could practically see the strings attached to his lips and tongue.

"Yeah, well, I saw Alden that night in the Hole. We, like, shared a joint together and then he split. He went one way and I went the other."

"Then what happened?"

"I don't know. He went to check out his hippie friends. Ask them what happened."

"Why didn't you say you were with Alden before?"

"We were doing something illegal. Smoking grass is illegal, right? Are you gonna bust me?"

"Not for that. Did you hear or see anything after you and Alden split up?"

"Naw. Just what I said before."

"Nothing at all?"

"No. If you want to find out something why don't you ask his hippie friends?"

"You're dying to know what they said, aren't you?"

The calming hand of Lynda Mayo fell upon her son's shoulder. Chezevski knew he had gotten in as close as he was going to.

Bartlesby stepped in. "I don't think any more questions will be necessary. If you want anything else you'll have to use a subpoena or arrest him."

Chezevski opened his vinyl Kensington P.D. folder and presented Bartlesby with a search warrant. Bartlesby read it.

"Everything is in order," he announced.

Chezevski paid no attention to him. He visited Mayo's room and took a T-shirt and a pair of shoes. Then he went to the shed out back and picked up the two shovels that were there, a spade, a pair of work gloves and a can of barbecue starter.

Bartlesby understood Chezevski's choice of objects, but he played it cool. No reaction from the downtown lawyer. For him it was a game, another case. It wasn't the same for Chezevski, and that made him feel inferior. He hated Bartlesby for it.

I WAS INSIDE the policeman's house. Naked with the policeman's daughter. It was hard to get comfortable. Even if the Sgt.-Det. was gone for the evening to a polka bash in the old neighborhood.

"He sent the dirt to Washington and they did some kind of analysis," Yvonne said. "It matched up. Why don't they charge him? Charge the fucker!"

Yvonne slammed the bed with her fist.

"What do they have on him?"

"Everything! The dirt was the same. The charcoal starter was the same stuff Mayo used to light his clothes. The gym shoes are the same size. And the ground from the shovels—the analysis is good within a hundred feet of any spot on earth. I don't get it!"

The record stopped. She got up and put on Disraeli Gears again:

> I'll stay in this place where the trains run through
> Stay in this place
> Where the shadows run from themselves...

She came back to bed. To talk about Alden's murder, she pulled the covers around her body.

"And I don't get this business in the papers, either!" she complained.

The Sgt.-Det. had opened a second front. He was playing politics now. He had made a statement to *Suburban Life* about how there was no prime suspect, a few scraps of evidence at best, and even less cooperation from the community. The result was consternation from the city fathers and grumbling from the parents who bothered to read the paper. But Chezevski wasn't aiming at them. He was gunning for downtown, the rust-colored Civic Center building with the bony Picasso bird sculpture out front, where the State's attorney for the County of Cook lived. Mr. Jerry O'Shaughnessy. A State's attorney who did not care for Kensington because Kensington voted against him and his party every four years like clockwork. A dog could have run against him and the voters of Kensington would have pulled the lever on the side of the dog. And now O'Shaughnessy was punishing Kensington for its voting behavior by refusing to let the case be prosecuted. In his frustration, Chezevski was trying to cause such a stink on the local level that the County would have to let the thing go ahead.

It was an ingenious idea. It did not work. The boys in the State's attorney's office were deafer than he was loud.

"You've done everything you can do," I tried to comfort Yvonne. "Maybe we missed something. Maybe your father's waiting for more evidence. He might have something up his sleeve."

Yvonne did not want to be comforted. She draped the sheet around her and got up and paced around the room. There was only one thing we had not done: go to the police and swear we had seen what we had seen, and beg forgiveness for not having sworn it earlier. We listened to that option hanging in the air, another noisy silence. I knew Yvonne wanted it.

She stopped pacing and stood in front of a vertical panel of Reynolds Wrap hanging on the wall. Behind the foil was a full-length mirror she had covered during a psychedelic mood. "The reflections from this are truer than mirror reflections," she had said. That was a long time ago.

Now she raised her hand and tore the aluminum foil off the mirror.

"This stuff is stupid," she said.

Then she dropped the foil and looked at herself naked for a long time, weighing her chances for when she got out in the world, seeing herself out of Kensington for the first time. It was a calculating look. It made me jealous.

It was almost a relief when the telephone rang and she hurried from the room.

"It's Flynn, for you. The phone's on the kitchen table."

I pulled on my shirt to be less naked in the policeman's house. I went through the living room to the kitchen. It was no different from any other kind of house. There weren't rifles hanging on the wall. The only time Chezevski touched a gun, Yvonne said, was to shoot obligatory target practice.

"Flynn the Loveless on the line."

"That's not my fault." I wasn't in the mood.

"Look, we have to go for a ride."

"But I'm over here."

"Look, it's about Blowy. It's good news. It's a letter. It was here when I came by from work. I have to read it to you. In person.''

Flynn and I had been distant lately, and Yvonne and I were at a dead end for the night. I told him okay.

"I'll wait at Fifty-Fifth and Gilbert, in front of Jack-in-the-Box hamburgers. Get me there.''

I went back to Yvonne's room. She was dressed and sitting on the bed. The same song was playing:

> You said no strings
> Could secure you
> At the station...

"Flynn wants to see me. He's all excited about something. A letter from Blowy. I'm sorry...''

"It's okay. You have to leave sooner or later.''

I walked down wide Fifty-fifth Street toward the corner of Gilbert. I didn't understand it. First I was jealous of guys she didn't have yet. Then I got up and left her bed. I just didn't want to see the end happen right before my eyes.

Jack-in-the-Box was one of those sawdust hamburger palaces where you drive in the mouth end and give your order, then drive out the ass end and your hamburger is ready. Flynn was in the parking lot, munching on a Boxburger.

He handed it to me and I smelled Yvonne on my fingers. I wished I had grown up learning to speak, instead of laying low. I might still be with her now.

"Important news,'' Flynn said with his mouth full. "That's why I asked you to come without your teddy bear.''

"She wouldn't have come out anyway.''

Flynn let it pass. He swallowed his burger.

"Let me read this to you. It's a week old but as fresh as we can get:

I was in-country when I heard there was a letter for me. Guess what? An invitation to testify at a Grand Jury, something I've never done before, and I've done a lot of new things lately. Great. You can run but you just can't hide. It's all because of that little dance with the trash basket on Main Street: they figure I'm a criminal, that's why they're sub-peenying me. What's the use? I've said everything I can about CA. If you think of anything new you say it for me, you're my interpreter. Shit, they fought to send me up here and now they're fighting to get me back. Right now I'd just as soon stay. There it is.

A little later...

I've been made to see the error of my ways. I've been made to see the whole thing as a gigantic R and R. I'm heading for the coast as soon as I can get clearance. No more There It Is for me.

"Fucking Blowy," Flynn exulted, "Baby's coming home to Daddy!"

He started Angel's motor and we backed out of the lot. "Now that most definitely calls for a raid on a pik-a-nik basket. But listen to this: no more sneaking around Miss Hooper's place. I've got myself all I need at home."

On the radio there was an oldie about wearing flowers in your hair. The Summer of Love and all that. It was amazing, the stuff they would play on AM once they had deemed it harmless. Flynn sang along, doing a parody, happy for once. Until we pulled up in front of his place.

There was a paper jammed into the frame of the screen door. It looked like one of those advertising flyers we used to deliver as kids for a penny a flyer. Except that we never delivered them at ten at night.

Flynn stood on the sidewalk and stared at the door.

"There's something I forgot to tell you, Boo-Boo," he began slowly. "Blowy made me next of kin. Blowy was sort of an orphan, and he... Go get that paper for me. I don't want to touch it."

I walked up to the screen door and pulled off the paper. It was from the United States Defence Department. I turned and held it out to Flynn.

"You open it."

I did. It was true. Blowy was dead.

I dropped the paper on the ground and nodded at Flynn. The messenger always has the hardest part to play.

Flynn let out a wail so high-pitched and weird I had to clap my hands over my ears.

"It's that fucking cop's fault! That fucking cop!"

I couldn't tell him any different. Blowy had been shot down on his way back to the coast. Back to Chezevski's subpoena.

I put my arms around Flynn. There was nothing to do. He was sobbing.

"Holy shit! Who's next? Who's gonna be next?"

Then a second later he went calm and flipped into crazy talk. That was the worst part of all. "Boo-Boo," he told me, "as sure as bears like honey we're going to have to make a vigil for this man. If we don't, nobody else will."

He pulled away from me and marched into his house. The paper was on the sidewalk. I went to pick it up, I don't know why, habit I guess. I stopped. I did not want to touch it, either. It didn't matter now. Let it blow through Kensington and spread the news.

Flynn came out with a bottle of Pleasant Moments blended American whiskey. He was sipping on it before we even got to the curb where Angel was parked.

"Come on, Flynn, I don't want you dead too. I *refuse* to let you do it."

"I won't do it," he assured me, "but I may die trying."

"No clichés, now. Let's go to Shawmut Park."

I don't remember what we talked about. Blowy's exploits. Then Flynn flashing bitter about me having Yvonne, and me having to tell him it wasn't my fault, she had just come to me, I had done nothing to deserve it. He flipping in and out of this crazy cartoon-character talk, Yogi and Boo-Boo, Fred and Barney and Wilma and Bam-Bam. I'm sure he wished he were on a TV screen somewhere in someone's rec room, flat as a pancake, away from all this pain, where all he had to do was talk, talk, talk.

Somewhere in the middle of the night I started getting bored with being called Boo-Boo and having a whiskey bottle referred to as honey. Flynn was beginning to mourn himself and forget about Blowy. I remembered I had to punch in at Star of Zion in another hour. I told him that.

"Work, jerk. Tomorrow's a natural day of mourning."

"I've got to go. Need money."

Flynn threw the keys at me. High. They hit me in the chin.

"If you want to profane Blowy's memory and go to work,

that's your soul. Let Angel look after it. Her tires are bald and her brakes are shot.''

He lay down on the ground. "I'm staying here."

Then he discovered how cold the dew was. "Forget it. Drive me home."

I had the keys; I had to drive. I settled in behind the wheel and tried to remember what to do. I looked out the windshield but could not see a thing.

"Some fucking vandals have spray painted the windshield," I reported.

We got out to investigate. "Fucking Chezevski! Fucking Mayo! They did this!"

I ran my hand along the windshield. "It's the dew. It's the goddamned dew!"

We were jubilant. Into the car again. We drove out of the park onto the approach to Ogden Avenue.

"The fucking lights are smearing again," I warned Flynn.

"Work the wipers! Work the wipers!"

I did. The button came off in my hand. I realized how much Pleasant Moments we had put away.

I also realized it was the moment to throw up. I went about preparing for it methodically. I stopped the car but something did not work right because we both went flying forward and kissed the dash. Suddenly the wiper blades started moving at top speed. I opened Angel's door and threw up a great amber stream of Pleasant Moments.

On his side Flynn was doing the same. "Only fucking thing we know how to do together any more: puke."

We got rolling again. From some malevolent corner of the sky dawn was creeping up. It was time to head for the packing house. I dropped Flynn off in front of his house. The telegram was still there, crumpled on the sidewalk.

"I didn't even get an honor guard of Marines to regret to inform me," Flynn lamented.

"Maybe because you weren't his parents."

"But I was his best friend! His . . . interpreter. He said so. He said so himself! And I still am! I still am! It doesn't matter if he's dead!"

He charged his front door and got into his house somehow. I drove on, leaving Flynn with his new obsession.

I got onto the expressway. Before I hit Harlem Avenue, two

great fiery suns came rising out of Lake Michigan, directly in front of me. It was going to be quite a day. I pulled over to throw up. That's how I made it to the Star of Zion: Austin, Central, Pulaski: puke. Every few exits on the Stevenson. Kedzie, California, Damen: puke. I don't think I'll ever forget that taste: Blowy's ghost and Pleasant Moments on the still-cool pavement. And the Angel of Death all fettered in rags following like a cop.

I walked up to the plant just in time to see the house rabbi kissing the wall of the Star of Zion. Lips to the Water Market! With all due respect to the Lord our God, I turned and threw up the last of the Pleasant Moments. Great. Ready for work.

I punched in and went to change into my monkey suit. Dried, gnarled and black, old Roosevelt was sitting in front of his locker. He was staring at a half-pint of bourbon. The DPs called him Rosenvelt because his job was to kosher the meat. He looked up in case I was some representative of authority.

"Shit! You look like you seen your ghost!"

He handed me his bottle, not even open yet. He must have been trying to decide whether to break the seal, and here was someone to do it for him.

"You need this," he told me.

"Like a hole in the head." I broke the seal. "I've just seen the ghost of my best friend."

Roosevelt shook his head sadly. "Happens all the time."

I drank: "Breakfast of champions!"

Everybody laughed. Suddenly I felt clownish. A kid drinking in the company of old men, trying to be like them. Conduct undignified on the first day of Blowy's death.

One of the DPs was shaking his finger sadly at me.

"Vonss you get in factor, you never leaf," he prophesied.

I opened my arms to take in the locker room. "This does not suffice me," I told him. "I'm gonna Exodus out of here real soon. You'll see, I'm gonna be a college boychik. A 2-s."

Slipped that curve right by you, didn't I, Uncle Moishe? A real spitter: a Haggadah-ball dipped in whiskey.

The usual day, the usual routine. Exploding sausages in maniac machines, scalded hands, nature abhorring the Cryovac, fat ladies calling my sexuality into question because I weighed less than they did, me avoiding the DPs, discomforting in their resemblance to my singing aunts and uncles.

I went down to the pay phone by the front office, and right

there on company time I called Flynn. Busy. Busy again. He must have kicked the phone off the receiver before he crashed. I tried Yvonne, for comfort: nobody home. I felt a great, alcoholic loneliness, as if no one would ever be home again when I called, and I would have to stay in this factory forever. *Vonss you get in factor, you never leaf.*

Toward the end of my shift, around three-thirty, I went looking for overtime, as usual. I helped Joe the Smoke move his cages of sausages in and out of the smoker, an hour at time-and-a-half. Then I spent another hour with Roosevelt hosing down the emulsifying equipment. He held the high-pressure hot-water hose under one arm so he could drink with his free hand. Alcohol had no effect on his character. He never spoke, he never staggered, he never got up or down. All his blood had been replaced with whiskey. A little more, a little less, it made no difference.

Around five-thirty I went in to see Red Watson. He was in his little foreman's cubbyhole, reading the *Defender*.

"Got anything else for me to do?"

"Don't want to go home, do you?" Red looked disapproving. "There's a truck from Dallas already supposed to be here. I got to wait on it. You wait too if you want to. You can throw a few boxes on it if it ever gets here."

"I'll wait."

"Don't you be waiting in the tavern. A young man ought to have other things to do. Tavern's an old man's place. Read a book or something. Improve yourself."

"Okay, Pops."

Red chased me out of his office. That's what the Star of Zion needed: a library. Something more than a few sticky copies of *Cherry Busters*. Maybe some cowhide-bound volumes of *The Jungle*. I went into the locker room. Joe the Smoke had changed into his street clothes. He was sharing a half-pint of sour mash with himself before going home to his wife. I helped him share it.

"Don't drink too much of that, now," he cautioned me, "it'll cut your legs right out from underneath you."

I promised to be careful. I took a little taste.

"This place is just one big ginhouse anyway."

And Joe the Smoke spat on the floor in defiance of health regulations.

At a little after six the Dallas truck pulled in. The driver was a stubby little guy with a shiny red face and a blond crewcut. In the Water Market, he stood out like a Martian. Cracker Cartage Incorporated. He scrambled up to the loading dock with a piece of paper in his hand. He squinted at it.

"This here Star of Zion? I'm looking for a Red Watson. Are you Red?"

"*Mr*. Watson. And this ain't no Baptist church, neither. This is kosher," Red boomed, as though he had personally received the Commandments.

Then came the usual Kasbah scene. Cracker Cartage besieged by kids selling bootlegged tapes of your favorite country stars, dealers selling uppers to speed his way home down South, a black girl in a blond wig selling her favors. That's what got Red so mad: the young black girl climbing in after Cracker Cartage, up into the sleeper. We started loading the trailer.

Halfway through the load I knew something was wrong. Maybe the first skid I'd set down wasn't flat. The whole load was off. Maybe the girl was in a hurry to get away from Cracker Cartage after she'd made her money, and hit some kind of hydraulic lever. I felt the air moving above me. I looked up and saw the top box two feet over my head tipping down and bringing the whole stack with it. And the stacks behind. It was a hypnotizing sight. My reflexes wouldn't fire in. In a trance I watched the wall come down, a slow-motion wave. It took Red's shouts and the first box hitting me to wake me up. I spun away but the cartons were falling faster and my leg got pinned underneath. I couldn't get my fall right. I heard a clear, sharp snap from under the boxes. *Not me. Not this time.* But it was. It really was. Before pain could take over, the survival instinct flipped in. My mind flew high over the trailer and the Water Market and I gazed upon my body far below in its distress, felt interest and pity, but knew no pain.

Red Watson's voice was close and gentle like a preacher's.

"I should have never let you work, I should have never let you work."

And he was digging, throwing off the weight, pulling me out. Then I was on the loading dock and he was sitting on me to keep me from moving.

"I should have never let you work, goddamnit, I shouldn't

have, it's my fault, you're going to be all right. Be all right, will you?''

And my mind answered him. It came down from its perch against pain to move both my feet and see there was nothing wrong with my spine. And lift my head to survey my body and find my legs were straight and unbroken.

It was going to be all right. I touched Red's shoulder and nodded.

Then the ambulance was there. The stretcher, the alcohol swab and the needle in the butt. Things ran together after that. Dark, anxious nuns at Emergency. *Kids*, one of them hissed as if it were a curse word. Then I was in bed and dreaming. In the dream I flailed my arms in struggle but was met with gentleness, for the water pitcher I knocked from the table did not crash to the floor as I deserved it to. It floated ceilingward and the water inside came flowing out like sparkling tears of silver, drops of enchanted quicksilver in the air.

I woke up with a wrapped knee. A Filipino nun was sitting over me.

''Did I say anything when I was under?''

She hesitated. ''Yes . . . yes, you did.''

''What did I say?''

''Things. Shameful things. Things about the body.''

I nearly jumped out of bed but a stab of pain kept me in place. Was that the way I would tell the truth, unconscious, under sodium pentothal?

''Just tell me what I said,'' I ordered the nun.

''I cannot repeat such words. But the doctor . . . he had to put your hand . . . there where is what makes a man a man . . . so you would believe him.''

I pulled the sheet over my head and shrieked with laughter into the chlorine-smelling mattress pad. Truth serum indeed!

I MADE THE ACQUAINTANCE of the good doctor on my first day out of the hospital. The good doctor was a brand of the singing aunts and uncles, the kind that read from the back of a book. Only he was a bit more distant, because he was a doctor. Dr. Bernard by name. He came visiting with his wife for Sunday supper, to sop up the brisket gravy with his bread. My father was eager to show off my injury. No one had ever been injured in the family before, and survived.

The doctor palpated my knee and shifted it back and forth.

"Easy trauma," he announced.

Everybody stared. "This young man is subject to easy trauma."

"We know that," my father muttered.

Dr. Bernard cocked his head to one side as if he had not heard correctly. Things medical were not to be taken lightly. Then he got to the point.

"How old is this young man?"

"This young man is of draft age," I offered.

"He is unfit for military service," the good doctor declared.

"Tell me more!"

"The nature of your injury makes you subject to easy trauma and, in my opinion, unfit for the rigors of military service. A debilitating reinjury is a very real possibility."

"Are you willing to put that down on paper?"

He looked at me as if I'd accused him of spitting on the Hippocratic Oath. Of course he was as good as his word.

It turned out that the good doctor had been an old WPA shovel leaner, way back in the old days. He had even once carried a Party card. But he had met and married a very beautiful woman, and decided he should make something of himself to be worthy of her. He became a doctor. He bought a large car with air conditioning. But secretly Dr. Bernard still leaned to the left of the shovel, and lately he had found himself a new vocation, a kind of mercy mission, creating a new generation of young men all subject to easy trauma for a wide variety of reasons.

The next week I went hobbling down to that squat, ugly pillbox on Ogden Avenue known as the Draft Board. I squirmed in pain every time the rotating fan blew hot air in my direction. I showed them the doctor's certificates and walked out of there declared Fit Only in Case of a National Emergency.

"This whole thing is one big national emergency," I said.

But, coward that I am, I waited until I had both feet firmly planted on the sidewalk outside to say it.

But a trauma did set in, and it was not an easy one. A trauma of exhaustion and loose ends that would not tie.

Flynn called up a few days after my visit to the Draft Board.

"Looks like the war's over."

"Come on, Flynn, just because I'm 4-F doesn't mean the war's over."

"For you it does."

Things went downhill from there. I added Bobby Flynn to the list of losses. Not dead. Missing in action.

We had the run of Yvonne's place. I could not do too much in bed, just lie back and try to keep my left knee out of the action. She was athletic and eager like before, but the wonderment had gone out of it. It was like she was in some kind of training.

We stopped talking about the case. No more Detective Yvonne overhearing Czech conversations. We wandered naked through the policeman's house, looking for clues about what to do next, avoiding the mirror in her room which showed us as we really were. Sometimes we watched the late innings of a Cubs game on the black-and-white TV.

THAT FALL I READ about it in the papers. Then Yvonne called me and told me everything she knew.

Chezevski had had to wait until O'Shaughnessy shot himself in the foot before the Alden case could go ahead. It was an election year and to O'Shaugnessy's secret regret, his office was on the line again, as it was every four years. Maybe he had been dropping in the polls; maybe he was looking for a monster mandate. He decided to include a gun battle with the Black Panthers in his campaign strategy. He personally directed the battle, which consisted of breaking down the door of their West Side headquarters before dawn, shooting a couple of them in their beds, then charging them with all kinds of capital offenses. But it did not take long before the federal authorities in charge of that sort of thing decided that the corpses' civil rights had been violated. Poor O'Shaughnessy found himself on trial. But the Cook County jury could not make up its mind whether a true civil rights violation had occurred. At the trial's end, a few days before the election, O'Shaughnessy was a free and vindicated man, expecting to be returned to four more years of unimpeded State's attorneyship.

But even Chicago voters would only stand for so much. When

the smoke cleared, the morning after the election, they had traded in the Mick for a Polack.

Otto Jenek was the brand-new State's attorney. Kensington had always supported his party, even before Jenek was born, and he rushed to reward them. No sooner had he finished swearing to uphold and enforce the laws of the great State of Illinois than the Kensington P.D. was visited by a flying wedge of State's attorney's office investigators and even an assistant State's attorney. After so many years of neglect, it must have been something to see. The case was alive again. The evidence was dusted off. The hairs, the accelerant residue, the fibers, the dirt from the front and back and footrests of the shovel, the burned clothing and shoes, all the lab reports. Kensington and her loyal voters were being rewarded a little too precipitously.

One winter day as Mayo was walking down Ashland Avenue minding his own business and thinking about nothing, an unmarked car with Fuzzy Travers at the wheel pulled up next to him. Chezevski got out and arrested Mayo on a homicide charge.

One hundred thousand dollars' bail got Mayo free again. He did not have to spend a night in jail. That should have been Chezevski's first warning sign.

Chezevski still did not have that elusive witness. But it was obvious to him that Mayo had done it—and he must have thought it would be obvious to a jury. There was Mayo's prophetic essay. The physical evidence. His reaction under questioning, the changing stories to fit the changing evidence.

It did not look that way at all to Harry Bartlesby. He was detached enough, and he had spent enough years in the slippery corridors of the County Court Building to know where the friendly judges lived. His client was not an amiable sort. Bartlesby did not want a jury trial with a succession of fresh-faced hippie types hinting at the psychopathic nature of his client's personality. He went for a bench trial and got it. He went for the defense-minded Judge Gallagher and got him.

The prosecution kicked off with the physical evidence. For three hours Chezevski talked blood and dirt and fabric and hair to place Mayo at the scene.

Chezevski was ready for a lunch break. Instead, Gallagher said to him, "Mr. Chezevski, I understand you're leaving immediately after this trial for a fishing trip."

"Yes, Your Honor."

Chezevski thought he was satirizing his evidence with talk of going fishing. But Gallagher really did want to talk fish.

"Florida Keys?"

"Yes, Your Honor."

"Good swordfish there. And marlin too."

And Judge Gallagher proceeded to tell the story of his and his wife's last fishing trip to the Keys.

Chezevski was wishing for lunch the way a sleeper wishes for the end of a nightmare. Helplessly.

Bartlesby counterattacked. He mentioned the previous contact between his client and the victim, which he called "natural." He mentioned the alibi supplied by his client's mother. Of course his client wore the same kind of shirt and shoes as were found burned in the Hole. A lot of people did. A lot of people had barbecue starter in their garages. And someone could have put the shovel with the dirt in his client's garage to frame him. Besides, the lab in Joliet had mishandled some of the soil samples, making them doubtful evidence at best.

And knowing that Judge Gallagher was an old O'Shaughnessy man from way back, Bartlesby cast discreet aspersions on the case being dusted off after so long, and not as a result of any new evidence or witnesses, of which there were none, but because of the vagaries of electoral politics.

Then he moved that the charge be thrown out on grounds of insufficient evidence. Judge Gallagher sustained the motion. The trial was over—before lunch. Bartlesby took home fifty thousand dollars for his work.

ONCE OVER THE WINTER I was back in Kensington from university to consult the good doctor about my knee. There were knee specialists everywhere, but he was ailing and I wanted to see him before it was too late.

I don't know why I went by Yvonne's place. There was no reason for her to be in town.

It was eight in the evening, maybe nine. I parked around the corner and walked up to her house. It was changed. The carport was now a fully enclosed garage. The walls were made of translucent corrugated-plastic siding, like huge, pale green, rippled potato chips. No wood or brick or anything that might keep out the cold.

From inside the garage I heard Yvonne's song, with its softly thudding bass line:

> I ran into such a sad time
> At the station...

The side wall of the garage had a small window, high up, more for ventilation than for light. I found a cinder block around the back and stood it on end. I don't know what I expected to see inside.

The Sgt.-Det. was sitting on a metal stool under a sixty-watt light bulb with a drink in his hand, staring at a rock. A big piece of jagged-edged concrete on a turned-over cardboard box in front of him. On display, like in a museum. Yvonne's old phonograph was plugged in next to him on an extension cord.

I knew that rock. That rock had broken up the Kensington Krazies and put an end to the sixties. Now that Chezevski had lost his case in court, it had gone back to being just another rock in the eyes of the law. He was free to keep it if he wished. As a souvenir.

I climbed off the cinder block and put it back carefully behind the carport. The carport that Chezevski had turned into a meditation room for himself and his rock. He picked it up, he weighed it in his hands. He went through the motions of trial. He interrogated it.

I got out of there in a hurry. I hoped for snow during the night to cover up my footprints, leading away from the garage, across the white lawn.

Independence Day

4

I was wrapping up my year of university in this college-town bar with a college-town-bar name: the Rusty Scupper. A year of being disengaged from reality, an enormous privilege I thought I had earned. Not only 4-F; 2-S too.

The Rusty Scupper had a down-home decor; whose home, I did not know. The establishment served beer in Mason jars. I had had to plead to get mine in a glass that any self-respecting drinker would not be ashamed of.

It was early May. I had been out of Kensington for ten months. Almost a year since Flynn had wished me death on Angel's bald tires, and I in turn had greeted the twin Chicago suns rising out of Lake Michigan with a great spew of Pleasant Moments vomit. Ten months was not enough to make me forget what a great waste we had made of things. Ten years would not have sufficed. As I had feared, Yvonne and I had come down with ghost disease. Infected by the spirit of Charles Alden. We no longer felt at ease with each other; we had nothing more to say. Her skin took on a different texture: dry and defeated and unyielding. As if the big adventure had been to coax the legal apparatus into charging Tom Mayo, and when it had, and the charges fell through, all the fun had gone. When the Sgt.-Det. had lost his case, I realized, his daughter and I had lost ours too.

Yet I was restless for Kensington-style reality when Yvonne's letter came that morning:

You ask me if I've been true, like you always do, my dear Vinnie. Let me put it this way: you're the only man I've ever witnessed a murder with. Kind of makes you special, doesn't it? Talk about the ties that bind . . .

And while we're on the subject, I had a call from the Sgt.-Det. last night. Remember Judge Gallagher? Of course you do. His son got murdered down in Florida recently. And the murderer got off on grounds of the insufficiency of physical evidence. Everything that goes down comes around, like Papa says.

Papa says a whole lot more things but a piece of lined paper can't hold them all. I think we're going to have to meet some time soon.

I knew about Papa, sitting in his garage with his rock on top of a box like a sick trophy, listening to music he could not have possibly understood. The image made me want to do something for him. Something more than be a cheering section on the sidelines.

Outside, the late spring warmth was burning off as the sun began to sink. I sat, moony and all poetic-looking, with my scrap of paper and a beer going warm and cloying in my conventional glass.

Tonight there were hippies at the Rusty Scupper. Untoward, I thought. A bar was for drinking, and drinking was a reactionary high. I recognized one called Rabbit, a white male Caucasian, and two female followers, Mona, a great big dumpling eater who could knock a man flat with the swing of one breast, and a whippet woman named Denie, dark and fine-featured and abundantly mustached.

Denie and Mona were rocking back and forth in the vinyl booth, moaning "O-o-rgasm!" Then they broke up in screechy laughter. The rumble under the floorboards of the Rusty Scupper was Wilhelm Reich spinning in his grave. Rabbit was not fazed. He began a discourse to the effect that only those individuals who did not wear underwear could lay claim to being liberated.

Listening to them, I felt righteous anger coming on, which I recognized as the prelude to ordering another drink. I did so. Then the evening news came on and I tuned out Rabbit and his hutch. The sound was low, as it always is in bars, but the pop-pop sound of TV gunshots caught my attention. On the screen above the bar, doll-like figures were being thrown around. I recognized war conditions, and how a tiny bullet can throw a human body into total, undignified disequilibrium before it has time to fall to the ground. But one thing on the screen did not fit in: the bodies were white, not yellow or brown. And they were dressed like me.

The cameraman must have been caught in the middle of the trouble. The figures were jumbled together, then the camera panned involuntarily to the sky. There was a flash of overexposed light. Then we got a good look at a clock tower. Midwest campus Gothic. It was America.

I stood up, put a hand out to turn up the volume, though the TV was above the bar. Suddenly a woman rushed into the Rusty Scupper. Her shirttail was out. She had been running.

"They're shooting us!" she cried. "They're killing us! My God, they're murdering our brothers and sisters!"

The Scupper went quiet. On the TV set the scene was still playing silently. No one knew what to make of her. *Bad acid*, I heard Rabbit mutter from the back of the bar.

The woman's eyes were enormous. She was living a nightmare. Desperate for some way to speak the unspeakable: they were killing us on our own ground. We were killing ourselves.

She looked at the silent TV. "There it is! There it is! Now you'll believe me!"

"Turn up the goddamned sound!" I shouted at the barman.

The bar went quiet as the announcer showed us the film footage again and told us the story of the Kent State shootings. Someone in the bar sobbed. Another protested that the shootings were unconstitutional, that we had the right to free and peaceful assembly. But most people just stood there. And as they did I could feel them growing smaller. They stood and watched, and shrank into themselves. Of course, they were angry at a government that would break the American covenant with them and start shooting them like brown or yellow people. But mostly they felt small and vulnerable because they could do nothing about it except watch it on TV.

There was a funeral silence. We were lamenting the end of the protest generation. Only Mona could not stand the stillness. She began to howl.

"The revolution's here! Get your shit together in the streets!"

She and Denie and Rabbit headed for the door. There were not too many takers for the revolution. Everyone stared at the television or the floor, feeling small and vulnerable and ashamed at being part of the victim class. It was a new sensation for most of them.

"Come on, people, get off of your seats!" Mona begged us. "Get your shit together in the streets!"

Then she whipped off her T-shirt and swung it around over her head. That helped swell the crowd a little. They pushed through the door and into the street. Taking off your shirt did not seem like a very revolutionary gesture to me.

The bar went back to being quiet, almost desolate, like after an explosion. A few patrons finished their drinks and wandered out, making as little noise as possible, as if they were afraid of being spotted and shot by the National Guard within them.

"Crazy kids," an all-day sipper sitting next to me said.

Then he went around the bar and turned down the volume on the TV set. I could not believe everything was going to go back to normal. Was this going to be the murder of Chuck Alden on a national scale? Everyone watching, knowing, but doing nothing, waiting around for the ghost disease to infect them and make their own and each other's bodies distasteful things?

The all-day sipper ordered a whiskey and set it in front of me. I saw why: I was the only other customer in the Scupper. I raised my glass and examined the lights through it: they were a pleasant, faraway color. The kind of haze around things that the all-day sipper sought.

Like an object lesson in the evils of alcohol, he had fallen asleep, very comfortable looking, in perfect balance on his high stool. I could hear the commotion the shirtless revolutionaries were making outside. The tear gas had crept into the bar, adding another irritant to the smoke and lethargic ventilation. I picked up the sipper's untouched shot, and like my father with Elijah's glass, threw it back. I patted my pants pocket and felt Yvonne's talisman there.

Outside in the street, people were getting their shit together, as Mona had wanted. There was more going on than I had imagined. Crackling bullhorns, the soft pop of a tear-gas canister, the glare of fire-truck flashers attenuated by smoke. I counted my whiskeys as I strolled down the main street of the student ghetto, up the hill toward the university where the trouble was. Perhaps three, or five. Nothing extravagant, honest. But enough to run the separate events of my life together. The shootings on TV in front of a nation of witnesses, the Sgt.-Det.'s moon face staring questioningly out the windshield of his Olds 88 as we waited in the darkness for him to pass, crouching in the scummy brush of the Hole until it got too late to help. Things may run together with alcohol, but associations are never random. If the pop and yield of a tear-gas canister makes you think of a human skull, this is no accident.

The ROTC building stood on the crest of the hill, where the main street ran into the campus. The crowd was dancing on the building's lawn. From broken windows in its limestone facade, smoky fires were burning, mostly plaster and lathe and paper. The fire trucks were parked on the street, their lights whirling around; the crowd would not let them get close to the blaze. The campus policemen stood with their arms folded next to the firemen. Workman's compensation was not generous enough to make them want to tangle with a crowd that size.

Then the town cops, the real kind, arrived to escort the firemen to the burning building. The cops flew out of their cars four at a time. They had never seen so many long-hairs from so close and they wanted to get their share. They started clubbing at the edges of the crowd as people took off. I saw Mona stream past, her shirt still off, bleeding from a gash on her forehead. *You are awfully near the front*, I reminded myself. I tried to retreat, but the crowd was too thick behind me. The police blindsided one long-hair, and his granny glasses went flying. Everyone scattered like ants on an anthill. The long-hair crawled toward his glasses with blood covering half his face. But the cop was greedy, he wanted more. He brought his club down again, but someone deflected his arm and he couldn't make the blow count. When his club arm was down two or three guys jumped on it and the cop had to bend with their weight or say goodbye to his arm and shoulder. He sank to his knees and someone kneed him from behind in the ass and he rolled over. He tried to roll to his feet but his arms got pinned under a half-dozen pairs of waffle-stompers. Then the horror began. The crowd was moving all around us, streams of people screaming and chanting, and there was this one spot of motionlessness where the horror was going to happen. I heard a sharp snap and saw the cop's plastic visor go flying. A woman leapt for his face, it could have been the wife of the long-hair with the granny glasses. Her fingernails were like claws and she was screaming and there was dirty spittle all around her mouth. She got at the cop's eyes with her fingernails, then I heard the cop scream. A long scream until he ran out of breath, then in the hush underneath the crowd noise I distinctly heard the sick loose pop and release of an eye getting put out.

I found myself on a street corner a block from the riot, slumped against a traffic light changing needlessly in the night. Adrenaline gave way to nausea. I had to get the night out of my system. I was on all fours, scratching around in the dirt. Then I found a twig on the ground and stuck its twin prongs down my throat. All those memory-killing drinks flew out of me.

THAT NIGHT, CLEANSED of the alcohol, I had a dream. It is not usually given to me to recall a dream with such clarity. I was in a great department store—it was Christmastime—with the towering tree, the tinkling music, the strings of lights. I knew I could pick out anything I wanted. But before I had the chance I was called outside. I passed through a set of double doors and it was another world. I understood I had been summoned outside to witness an accident. I heard my name called twice and looked in the direction of the voice. There were the sounds of an automobile accident, the tires squealing, the windshield shattering. Two bodyless pairs of legs ran from the scene. My name echoed over the sound of the impact and I remembered thinking: It is not I who caused that accident, I am right here, not over there.

What woke me was the sound of the driver's chest being crushed by the steering wheel of his car.

I looked around and saw I was in my apartment, on the living-room couch. I did not remember lying down there, and felt that instant of panic when you wonder just how much you might have missed of the night before. I closed my eyes and saw flames from the burning building. When I opened them again I had decided it was time to return to the witness box we called Kensington.

"NOW YOU'RE WORKING FOR the forgetfulness squad," Yvonne told me straight off when we met. "I'm trying to make people remember and you're trying to forget."

"I am *not* trying to forget. I came back. I called you."

Our reunion had not started very well. It took a turn for the worse when I told her what I had had to do that day, my first day working for Kensington Streets and Water. My assignment had been to take a load of garbage to the dump. Broken sewer tiles, dirt, chemical sacks from the water-filtration plant. The dump, it turned out, was the Hole. I was helping the other side fill up the Hole. It used to be a joke among us: filling up the Hole. Now I was doing it.

"What do you want me to do? Commit civil disobedience my first day on the job?"

"Just drive somewhere."

"Anywhere in particular?"

Yvonne did not answer.

"How about Mr. Wrablik's rose trellis?"

"Leave that alone, would you?"

That was an unrealistic suggestion and I paid for it. I drove. I drove up and down Ogden Avenue. Over the Shawmut Park bridge four times.

"You can't just dump anything in a dump," I told Yvonne, as if she were interested. "They have a little dump policeman in a shed and there's a fence around the whole thing. We keep dumping in the dump and the dump keeps swallowing it up and not getting filled up. There's this kind of sinkhole with water at the bottom that they can never fill up. They're going to try and build houses on top after it's filled. Imagine the basements when it rains!"

There would be more than water in the basements. There would be bad dreams. The ghost of Chuck Alden seeping into the houses like a poison gas.

On our third trip down Ogden Avenue, I suggested, "Let's go to the Old Praha. I'm homesick for a Bohunk bar."

"No. My father will be there. Look! Slow down!"

I slowed down in front of the place and spotted the Olds 88 in the parking lot with the other heavy powerful Bohunk cars. The Sgt.-Det. was not in the Old Praha at all. He was sitting in his car, looking at the bar, wondering if he should go inside.

I accelerated through an amber light. "That gives me the creeps."
"Ogden Avenue's off-limits now."
That was a shame. I liked the oak-paneled bars and the copper-tinted mirrors and the way the bartender never spoke to you unless you let on you wanted to talk. I headed south toward McCook and the paint factories with their sharp limburger-cheese smell. There were bars there for the Mexicans who lived in the trailer parks.
"That's all he ever does: drive, drive, drive."
"Where does he go?"
"How should I know? In circles, I suppose."
We drove on into gloomy McCook. Before we got to the trailer camp I turned onto Fifty-Fifth Street. I did not feel like having to fight the first Mexican who came along and his thirteen switch-blade-bearing brothers, because Yvonne would be the prettiest girl in the tavern. Kensington never looked so hollow and wasted under her rust-inhibitor sky. I had never seen her so empty, neither city nor country, a collection of little brick bungalows and old wooden houses and jerry-built ersatz ranch and colonial houses, each jealously guarding its fifty-foot frontage on a crumbling residential street. Nothing good could ever come from this place.
"My father's not a good cop." Yvonne talked at her reflection in the windshield. "He doesn't know when to let go. All he does is think about the case. It's making him crazy. He tried 'talking it out'—now even cops have sensitivity sessions. It didn't work."
"Everything that goes down comes around," I reminded her. "Why doesn't he just let it come around?"
"That's his motto, only he doesn't follow it."
"And now we're going to help it come around, is that the plan?"
Yvonne shrugged and stared at the road as if it were not the one-thousandth time we had driven down it. This silence was new for Yvonne. A year ago she applied herself to every situation, every sight we saw together. Now she sat in silence and calculated revenge and would not say what kind.
"You know what the plan is," I said. "Memorial Day, the carnival in the empty lot out behind the Farmers' Market. Everyone will be together and we'll decide what we're going to do. Everyone—Patti, Flynn, Stotl, the whole bunch."
I turned on the radio. The Cubs were trailing in late innings

in Saint Louis. Nothing new there. I went down to the other end of the dial and picked up Big Bill Hill's Shopping Bag Show. He was telling one of his jokes about clothes. What's a shift? A dress that don't fit a woman nowhere else but her shoulders. Everyone in the studio laughed. Then he remembered to play some music and his R and B carried us along. I held onto the steering wheel and we just naturally found ourselves over by the ex-Hole. I pulled up by the wire fence and cut the motor. Across the dump was the water tower. It read, "Fuck off and die from the class of '70."

I tried to pull Yvonne closer but she would not slide across. What was automatic last year was a matter for negotiation now. The first skirmishes in a new war at home: the war between the boys and the girls.

I didn't force it. I stuck to business. Krazy business.

"Have you gotten hold of everyone for this picnic?"

"It's done. I know where everyone is. Everyone but Lo. She moved to Seattle and opened a dress shop," Yvonne said.

"Don't they have information in Seattle?"

"She got married. She changed her name."

"God, the misery continues! Imagine... Forget it—don't imagine. So who's in on the carnival?"

"You and me. Stotl and Patti Schmidt. And Flynn."

"You think they'll go for it?" I asked.

"I've tried out the idea. I didn't exactly talk about talking. But they're all willing to go on a Ferris-wheel ride together."

"I would have voted for bump-'em cars. What are they like now?"

Yvonne shrugged. "You'll judge for yourself."

"Don't forget: we don't judge. It's not cool. We just let things be. Right, Yvonne?"

YVONNE CALLED ME THE evening of the Ferris-wheel ride.

"I'm picking you up in my Daddy's Olds."

It gave me a case of the creeps. Were there truth sensors built into the dashboard? Would it be like under pentothal, where you felt the need to tell all?

When I got into the car I said, "I'd better feel underneath for hidden microphones."

I put my hand under the seat and touched something hard. It was not a listening device. It was a talking device: a half-drunk pint of bourbon.

"See why we have to help him? He never drank before."

"Everybody's got a reason." I took a pull from the bottle. "I drink to setting your father free."

"Please, put it away. I don't need two like that."

"Poor long-suffering Yvonne." I stowed the bottle where it belonged. "Have no fear, I smudged my fingerprints."

The Farmers' Market had no farmers. It was actually a dwarf shopping center on Forty-Seventh Street in Kensington, with an enormous parking lot that seemed to be designed for teaching people how to drive. The carnival was set up behind the Walgreen's. Flynn, Stotl and Patti Schmidt were sitting on Angel's front fender. A year had not changed them. Flynn was still pudgy and pug-nosed and loveless. Stotl's hair was a little shorter. You could see his vague blue eyes under his bangs. Patti Schmidt was in stable but critical condition, in a steady state of self-destruction. She would probably outlast us all.

We got out of Yvonne's car. Flynn snapped to attention.

"Officer Chezevski, reporting for duty!" He flipped a mock salute.

"Long time no see, Yogi Bear."

We shook hands.

"Are you ready for the fun house, Boo-Boo?"

"I am the fun house," I told him.

"Funny, I thought you were the spook house."

"Well, Flynn, I see everything's normal between us again."

"Normal's my middle name." He motioned to Yvonne. "Deputy Dawg called out the posse here tonight. We're eager to ride off into the sunset but we don't know where it is."

"I think the idea is to get onto that big wheel. Then everything will become miraculously clear."

We walked toward the carnival installation. It was a relief to do the Kensington Krazies again, even if it was a little contrived. It was like speaking the same language. We looked at the carnival rides. Most of them were for the under-ten set. The only one that interested me was the bump-'em cars. We could all get on and bash into each other without anyone really getting hurt.

Flynn was interested in the loop-the-loops. I saw why. Making three rings would win you a plush Yogi Bear.

"Come on, Daddy, win it for me. You got an arm."

"I can only hit a target from ninety feet out. Try it yourself, you're more motivated."

"I hate to lose. Forget it."

To console him I bought him a great big disgusting cotton candy. He grabbed a gob of it and crushed it in his hand until it was no larger than a pea.

"You think you've got something," he explained, "then it turns out to be this."

He opened his hand and the little spitball of cotton candy rolled onto the ground. We stepped up to buy our tickets for the Ferris wheel. The attendant checked us out, three guys and two girls in a car for six.

"You hold on," he said, "I'll get you another girl."

"That's all right." Flynn patted the empty seat next to him. "This seat is taken. You just can't see the guy sitting here."

The attendant looked at Flynn and saw he was serious. He slammed the car door and jerked us up a level.

"Jesus Christ, Flynn, did you have to?"

"Blowy's here," he said calmly. "I'm going to tell you what he says."

Flynn was like a child with an imaginary playmate. You couldn't see him, nobody could, but if you accidentally stepped on him you were in for trouble. The carriage rocked upward. The sky was hazy, with one of those long, drawn-out summer sunsets that never seems to end. I admired the view below, the ant people scurrying in and out of stores, buying things, trying to loop the loops and win a stuffed bear.

We climbed the wheel. I started to talk.

"We're up here on this great wheel of fortune because some of us think we should reopen the Mayo case. I think you all remember who Tom Mayo is. Well, I happen to believe that a general wave of insanity has come over us because of him."

"Blowy thinks so too," said Flynn.

"I've never had the dead on my side before," I told Flynn,

"but so be it. Does anyone have any opinions on whether we should reopen the case? Patti, you knew Chuck in a way we didn't.''

"I think about him in a way you don't. Here, I drew some pictures.''

Patti reached into the pocket of her boy's-size Sears work shirt and took out a half-dozen sheets of paper folded into tiny squares. We all watched passively, wondering what kind of stage business she was going to unleash on us now. She unfolded the squares and passed them around like after-dinner mints. Real proud of her stigmata. *Myself*, the first paper read. A tangle of stick figures like kids draw, except these had great distended bellies. The kind of assignment shrinks get their loony patients to draw for them.

I was not in the mood for show and tell. "I know I don't have much imagination,'' I told her, "but I don't see anything about Chuck in here. We're trying to figure out what to do about Chuck, remember?''

She gave me a superior smirk and handed me another paper. There were two figures in a bed with some kind of mystical aura rising up above the backboard. Primitively drawn so you could see the bodies underneath the sheets.

"This is Chuck for me,'' Patti stated.

Yvonne was impatient. "What does this have to do with the case?''

Patti Schmidt basked in the glory of the moment. Holding everyone in suspense at the top of a Ferris wheel, wondering what the crazy woman would do next! The control trip of craziness was never so clear to me.

I handed her pictures back. A year ago I would have coddled her craziness for fear she would run to the cops and make us all accessories. Not now. Now I wanted to strip her of her power.

"What this means,'' I interpreted, "is that Patti is not participating in the discussion for the time being.''

"Go get 'em! Clip those Elephant Ears!''

I did not need Flynn's encouragement. "Watch out or I'll sit on your imaginary friend,'' I told him.

I turned back to Patti. "We'll get back to you when it's time to vote. Now, the way I see it is that we have to decide whether to witness against Mayo or not.''

"And if so, how,'' Yvonne put in quickly.

"Flynn? This ride lasts five minutes. Let's decide."

"I say we talk. Blowy does too. Though he has ideas on how to do it that I couldn't possibly have."

"Yvonne?"

"We are witnesses. That's the way it is."

"Stotl?"

"Everything's going along all right, why change it? I mean, I feel bad for Alden and all that, but it's too late to change it."

"Patti, give us your opinion. You were there. You have to have an opinion on what happened."

"I can't talk to policemen and judges and people like that. I have to take care of my mother, she needs me. I won't do it, whatever you say." Then she turned on Flynn violently. Good thing she did not have a Teflon frying pan. "Besides, it's not true you know what Blowy thinks. You're just making all that up. You don't really know!"

I had to laugh. Nothing offended Patti Schmidt like another person's craziness. She was afraid of getting outflanked.

"All right," I summed up, "two for, two against," though I was tempted to count Blowy as a separate vote. Why not believe in ghosts?

"That puts your den mother in the position of tie breaker. I vote for talking and that's three against two. Not too bitter, Carl?"

Stotl shrugged. "It's your funeral. I'm innocent. Remember, you used me to find the corpse."

"Don't say *corpse*, Stotl, it's not polite," Flynn scolded him.

"All right," I pushed on, "we've decided to turn Mayo over to the cops. How do we do it?"

"Objection, honorable den mother," Flynn spoke up. "We did not agree to turn him over to the cops. We agreed to *witness*. Not the same thing."

"I like that word," Stotl said, "it's like we're our own police."

"Blowy wouldn't have put it that way," Flynn said, "but it appeals to him a lot. It appeals to the self-sufficient side he's been able to develop lately. He never thought a burned-out flower child could come up with something that good."

"Chew the wazoo," Carl offered.

"As the builder of consensus I'm happy that the handsome young man with the name no one can say has gotten into the swing of things," I went on in a Krazy vein, "but since you voted no you don't really have the right to speak. Isn't that in the rules? You're either in or out.''

"That's a hell of a way to build consensus," Stotl complained.

"You guys still think this is a joke!" Yvonne yelled at us, and her voice was carried away into the air. "All it is is talk, talk, talk with you! You want to turn Mayo in? You want to witness—whatever that means? Let me tell you where we stand and we'll see if you still want to laugh. Let me give you a lesson in law. We lost the case against Mayo last fall in the courts. So it doesn't do any good to stand up and witness because you can't try him twice on the same charge. Come on, don't you watch TV—double jeopardy and all that? The only charge against him now is violating Alden's civil rights, and that won't work because Alden's white. So don't dream about an anonymous telephone tip—it's too late!''

Flynn put his hands to his temples like he had a bad headache. "Stop her, she's making me feel guilty. You're sleeping with her, Elephant Ears, stop her.''

"I can't, I've lost my privileges. Besides, what she's saying is true.''

"And the second thing, the poetic-justice thing, because I know you're all poets, is that the trial no longer exists. You want to know what was said, what evidence was put forward? Forget it! The very mention of the trial was wiped off the books through a legal maneuver called expungement. If you've got a first offender, a kid, and he's acquitted, the lawyer can petition to have the whole thing wiped off the books. And that's what happened. As far as the court knows, Mayo was never even tried!''

"They can't expunge people's minds," Stotl protested.

"I don't know about that. It looks to me they have.''

We were nearing the top of our second turn. I looked down.

"Now that you've told us all that," I said to Yvonne, "we might as well get off here.''

"I'd come with you," Flynn said, "except Blowy doesn't want to.''

"What happens when you don't agree with your imaginary playmate? One of you has to go.''

"I do the only reasonable thing: I go along with him.'' He smiled sheepishly.

I turned to Yvonne. "You underestimate our thirst for action.

Did you get us up here on this Ferris wheel just to teach us about double jeopardy, and how history got rewritten right under our noses, and not expect us to do anything about it? All right, we blew legal action. But we still have paralegal action.''

"Blowy likes that!'' Flynn said gleefully. "Anything that's got 'para' in it he likes.''

"Except *paratrooper*, I bet.''

"I don't see what paralegal action can be.''

"You don't know how it could help your father and his problem with the hidden speaking devices,'' I completed Yvonne's thought.

"Paralegal action!'' Flynn actually clapped his hands together like a child.

"We'll capture the objective,'' I said.

"And hold it.''

"I wouldn't hold that thing with rubber gloves,'' Yvonne spat.

"You have to,'' I explained to her. "You're in on it. This is your idea. We're gonna help the Sgt.-Det. one way or another.''

"The Kensington Krazy Marine Corpse,'' Flynn announced.

"But what are we going to *do*?'' Yvonne insisted.

"I'll think of something,'' I told her. "Trust me.''

At that Flynn howled with laughter.

The ride was over. Just below, at ground level, the attendant was bringing the cars down one by one and opening the doors for people. It was taking too long. I jumped from the car while it was still on the way down. If you're going to hit the pavement, why waste time waiting for the shock, right?

I HAD RESPONSIBILITIES. I had full-time employment driving trash from Kensington's Streets and Water and dumping it in the ex-Hole. A social mission, community action for the common good. I could not spend weeks on the road finding Tom Mayo. I got on the phone.

Mrs. Lynda Mayo picked it up on the other end. Yvonne looked on disapprovingly. Flynn jammed a fist in his mouth to keep from screaming with laughter like a monkey in Monkey Jungle.

"This is Blowy Bloedell,'' I told her. "I'm a friend of Tom's and I've been away in the service. Is Tom there?''

He wasn't.

"Do you know where I can find him?"

She did. She told me. Tom had gone to work in a big factory in a little factory town on the other side of the state line in Wisconsin.

I hung up.

"She told me everything. It was a snap. I can't believe it. People will say anything over the phone to strangers."

"When you've had your case expunged," Yvonne said solemnly, "you've got nothing to hide."

It was true. Mayo had the law on his side. We were the ones going outside it now.

ON THE FIRST DAY of the long Fourth of July weekend, Yvonne and Flynn and I were driving the I-90 through the soybean fields to Wisconsin. Another Kensington Krazy errand, with Angel as the faithful vessel. The errand lent us energy, as once getting Mayo charged had done; perhaps it would even keep us from flying apart a little while longer.

We traveled together in the name of the errand. If asked, we would each point to our personal reasons. Flynn would say he was doing it in the name of Blowy, his imaginary playmate, supposedly doomed to Nam by the Mayo business, but actually doomed by his inability to resist. I would say I was doing it for Yvonne, with whom I skirmished nightly to be let inside. Yvonne would claim it was for her father. The truth was that we were doing it because we had missed the first chance to take a stand back when it could have meant something.

All around us was the country. I knew nothing about the country, except that something called nature lived there. I knew nothing about nature either, except that you were supposed to sit back, in the middle of it, and all your worries would miraculously quit you. Nature, apparently, made you a better person. Perhaps we should have stopped the car right there, gotten out and wandered through the fields.

Once in grade school, we took a field trip to see nature. To a farm, actually. We watched the chickens pecking in the farmyard, but when we strayed too close to the cow pasture, the enormous cows came galloping over to stare at us with their big empty black eyes. We were so terrified we ran back to the bus and spent the rest of the afternoon safely inside with the chewing-gum smells.

The landscape rose and fell, gently and orderly, the midwest plains perfectly useful in every aspect. Inside those houses shiny with aluminum siding, controlled lives were being led, in accord with the landscape. I think I was actually envious of them.

Just before Rockford, the I-90 turned straight north into Wisconsin. Flynn was at the wheel. One hand on the wheel, the other on Yvonne's hand. I smiled to myself. Flynn the Loveless planning to use the confusion of the moment to dash through and capture love. I took Yvonne's other hand.

We drove past the big Chrysler plant that had had a wall sucked out a few years back during the Good Friday tornado. I had been on this same road that day, going to Rockford, a few miles from the plant. The rain was reflected in the headlights, so hard was it falling that afternoon. I found a bridge and drove into the ditch underneath it and stopped. The car rocked on its chassis; I thought I felt it leave the earth for an instant. I got out and lay flat in the ditch as I had been taught to in Mrs. Kovacs' disaster drills. All around, the storm roared like a freight train. I waited to be spared and I was, and so the afternoon became a memory, not the end of memory, but with a sour taste to it like the catch of vomit in the back of the throat, the taste of a spoiled childhood.

We crossed the line into Wisconsin. A bright early July afternoon, with Yvonne buffering two men's hands with equal pressure. Kensington Krazies, rest in peace. If only we could have.

FIFTEEN MINUTES LATER we pulled into the lunch-bucket town where Tom Mayo was staying. We were in beer country. At every corner was a friendly tap with a welcoming neon sign.

"Look at that one. The Doll's House. Ibsen in Wisconsin. Let's have a look."

The bar was so dim we had to feel our way toward a table. I could not see whether we were the only ones there, but it felt like it.

The bartender came around to take our order.

"Should I have a Rolling Rock or a Slippery Rock?" Flynn wondered out loud.

The bartender neglected to laugh. The Doll's House did not look like a place where very much was funny. Very Ibsenesque.

"How come this place is called the Doll's House?" I asked the barman.

"The owner's name is Mr. Dahl. I'm him. And I don't carry any Rolling Rock. I only have Wisconsin beer here."

"A Pabst," I said.

"An Old Style."

"Hamm's."

I should have known Flynn would order Hamm's—on the TV it was advertised by a bear.

"One Ribbon, one Style, one Hamm's."

The bartender went away. I felt grateful that Flynn did not order something for Blowy.

"If we're planning to do something here," Yvonne warned, "maybe we should be more discreet."

"That's right. A little procedure to avoid detection by the police."

"I thought we *were* the police," I told Flynn.

"Some police," Yvonne sniffed.

The bartender came back with the beers. They were too cold. I thought I spotted ice in mine.

We clinked our bottles together. "To righteousness," I proposed.

"What's that?"

"All Flynn knows about righteous is 'You've lost that lovin' feelin','" Yvonne said.

"Don't be cruel," I told her. "Anyway, you lost it first."

"What's righteousness?" Flynn wanted to know again.

"Righteousness," I decided, "is when you do a wrong thing for the right reason."

We drank to that. It was something we all could agree on. Icy or not, the beers soon disappeared. We got another round. By then I could make out the inside of the Doll's House. At the back of the bar was a lit-up Hamm's Sky Blue Waters clock, with a kinetic effect that made the river below the clock look as if it were perpetually flowing. Underneath was a little bandstand where they probably played hurtin' music on the weekends. You listened to it, had a few beers, then went home and hurt somebody. Along the back wall were a few pensioners. They poured their beer very carefully and watched the bubbles with heightened interest, a sure sign they had been in the Doll's House all day.

This was a skilled workers' town. People walked around with micrometers and sheafs of blueprints sticking out of their pockets. Mayo had no skills but his job did not require any. He was a night watchman in the big plant in town that made diesel engines. Mayo dressed as a cop—I couldn't wait to see it. Self-important in his play-cop uniform and play-cop hat, making the rounds, stopping at all the watchman stations and turning the key in the round leather-covered clock he had strapped on him. Pulling on locks, checking his perimeter, keeping an eye out for enterprising workers smuggling parts out of the plant so they could build their very own twenty-four-cylinder diesel engines in their basements. Saying things like "Roger" and "ten-four" on his play-cop radio, then going back to his guardhouse to flip through a pussy magazine and jerk off into the wastebasket.

I finished the second Ribbon. The most fitting punishment would be to leave Mayo exactly where he was, a security guard walking his rounds for the rest of his natural life. But we were not going to allow that. We were going to intervene. We were going to substitute unnatural for natural justice.

Flynn was signaling me from across the table. "Boo-Boo, we're here and everything but I don't know what to do next. That makes me depressed. What's the strategy?"

"We'd better plan something," Yvonne echoed him.

"There is no strategy," I told her and Flynn. "We'll do what we said we would at the fun fair: we'll capture the objective."

Flynn had his money out. "To do that we'd better reconnoiter."

He signaled to the bartender with a ten-dollar bill. "Two Ribbons, two Styles, two Bears."

Shades of Chuck Alden talking ducks and bunnies. A very unpleasant coincidence.

When we got outside Yvonne said, "We'd better get a place to stay."

"I still say reconnoiter."

"I go with Flynn." I was not ready for the business of choosing a room. Of who was going to sleep where, or with whom, or at all.

We had no trouble finding Mayo's factory; we just followed

the smokestacks. The plant stretched on forever. When you stood at one end of the installation you could not even see the other.

"What are we supposed to do with this?" Yvonne asked.

"Mayo works here," Flynn stated the obvious.

"I bet he's not the only one."

We drove slowly along the length of the plant. Some of the panels of glass still had blackout paint from World War Two, when they made tank engines here and were afraid of the Germans. A railroad spur line intersected the street and ran into the plant grounds. A half-dozen men were lashing a tarp over an enormous diesel engine that had been lowered onto a flatcar.

"Pretty impressive," Yvonne said. "Bigger than us."

"That's the industrial-romance thing," I told her. "Mayo isn't part of that."

"Look, here's where he lives."

Flynn slowed the car in front of a guardhouse, a little wooden shack with windows all around. Inside were rent-a-cops watching the flow of men and goods and looking at ID cards. None of them looked like Mayo. They were scrawny, dried-out codgers waiting for retirement. They looked like scarecrows in their baggy uniforms.

"How are we going to find him in all that?" Yvonne asked.

"We'll ask," I said. "You keep acting like Mayo's a runaway criminal. You're the policeman's daughter, you should know. He was found innocent. He *is* innocent. Nobody cares if you ask questions about an innocent man."

I turned to Flynn. "You'll remember I stowed a suspicious-looking bag in the back. Pull down this alley. I'm going to spring the latch."

Flynn started up Angel and pulled around the back of a restaurant called Mr. Bill's Dynamite Ribs.

"It smells good back here. I'm in the mood for food."

"Wait in there with Yvonne; I'll be right back."

I opened Angel's tailgate and got out my Kensington gym bag with the great seal of a lion smoking a pipe on it. Poor cross-country team. It had never been the same without us. I got my Streets and Water uniform out of the bag, brown pants and a brown two-pocket shirt with "Vinnie" written across the right pocket in green thread. Green and brown, my favorite colors. I undressed and got into the uniform in the front seat.

"You don't look like a worker for shit," Flynn complimented me.

"You wouldn't know what a worker was if it came along and bit you in the ass," I returned the compliment. "I'll have you know this is a bona fide Kensington Streets and Water uniform. If you don't watch out I'll brain you with my Beef Boners and Sausage Workmen of America union card!"

I slipped one of those ugly plastic pencil-and-screwdriver holders into my right shirt pocket to cover the "Vinnie."

"You kids order me a Mr. Bill special with plenty of hot sauce. I'll be right back."

I walked out of the alley and across the street to the guardhouse. I put on my Star of Zion walk: don't rush me, I'm paid by the hour. A rent-a-cop came out of his cage to check my ID. He carried no weapons, just a flashlight and a radio.

Before he could ask me anything I said, "Is Tom Mayo on now?"

The rent-a-cop was a shriveled fifty-year-old with a prematurely lined face. All around were people who really knew how to do things. All he knew how to do was read ID cards.

"I don't 'spect so."

"He wants some information from me. When's his shift?"

When in doubt, use a big word like "information." The rent-a-cop went into his guardhouse and came back with a sheet of paper.

"I can't read too good on account of my not having my glasses," he said. "This here's our schedule."

I took the paper and ran my finger down to "M." Mayo, Tom, 10:00 PM to 6:00 AM. The graveyard shift. Just fine for ghosts.

I gave it back to him. "Thanks."

"Should I say you came by?" the guard asked.

"Sure."

Then I walked away nice and unhurried for my Mr. Bill's special.

Flynn and Yvonne were sitting on the same side of the booth. There was a place set for me on the other side.

"I hope you guys are good at killing time," I said.

"Kill time before it kills you," Flynn got philosophical.

"Mayo works from ten at night till six in the morning. We've got all afternoon, all evening and all night to kill."

"We can always reconnoiter," Flynn said helpfully.

The rib platters arrived. The hot sauce was dynamite, just like the sign said.

"What does Blowy think we should do?"

Flynn looked genuinely surprised. He had forgotten all about Blowy. "He doesn't think anything. The dead don't come in until they're absolutely needed."

We paid and drove back along the main drag toward I-90 to look for a motel, and ended up choosing the one with the fewest painted deer and leprechaun statues on the front lawn. The Dairyland. Like a conscientious young couple, Yvonne and I inspected the room while Flynn the Loveless crouched on the floor of the car. There was a fold-up bed on wheels in the closet. I wondered who would get it on this night of three in a room.

I paid in advance and wrote Blowy's name in the register book. I had caught ghost fever too. We were all pretty young, it seemed to me, to be putting our trust in ghosts.

"It's time to practice our strategy," I said, "which right now is to kill time. I thought I spotted a place called the Zoo Gardens."

Yvonne and Flynn made animal noises.

"Lock me up inside," Flynn wished.

We got in the car again and found the Zoo Gardens. It did not live up to its name. We were the only animals there. The place had big soft armchairs that made it impossible to put your elbows on the table. It was a place for fifty-year-olds to discuss the difference between their second and third divorces.

An embalmed barman appeared who belonged to the reformed-alcoholic school of bartending.

"What can you drink in a place like this?" Flynn wondered out loud.

"I'll have a brandy Alexander."

"Give me a grasshopper," Flynn got into it.

Yvonne ordered a dream boat.

"There is no such drink," the embalmed bartender told her.

"No? Then give me a shot of bar bourbon and a Ribbon back."

There was the sound of sugary liqueurs slopping into electric blenders. The bartender went to work. He had obviously mixed a lot of colorful drinks in his time.

A grasshopper turned out to be large, creamy and emerald in color. Flynn took a taste of it.

"Foul," he said, then elbowed the glass over the edge of the table. The spilled green drink on the mauve shag rug was like a bad acid trip right there at our feet. The bartender saved us from further hallucinations by asking us to leave.

I hate to let alcohol go to waste, no matter how it tastes. I gulped my brandy Alexander on the way out. It tasted like melted Dairy Queen after a Little League game you'd lost.

We stood out on the street and watched the sun go down, which it was doing very slowly. I hated to wait, especially when I did not know what I was waiting for.

"If there was only something to *do*," Yvonne lamented. Then she brightened up. "We rented that motel room, so we might as well use it. They've probably got a color TV."

"The wide world of sports," Flynn smirked.

The sport was whose craziness was going to win and Flynn and I were the contestants. Yvonne was not the main stakes, even if having a perfumed girl in the summer heat with her long hair blowing in your face sharpened the blades. The sport was whose talk were we going to talk. Who would get to drive. Forget Chuck Alden, forget the decency of helping the Sgt.-Det. who had gotten into a case deeper than he was. Let's avenge an imaginary playmate, let's go for a ride, let's shoot off some Fourth of July fireworks. Let's see who dangles the car keys from his big finger.

At the Dairyland Inn we turned on the air conditioner and the TV. The sun had burned through the curtains all day and the room was unbearable. Flynn took off his shirt and flopped on the Jell-O bed. Flynn the loveless, pudgy and pasty-skinned and weighing too much. Yvonne dropped onto the bed too, and I watched her breasts move under her white shirt. I kicked off my boots.

"Beer," said Flynn. "We forgot to pick up beer."

The weather came on the local news presented by Eric Jonsson. Velcome to Visconsin. Summer on the Great Plains, high of ninety-five, low of eighty.

"Thirsty weather."

"Tell you what: I'll go get the beer. I could use a walk, we've been in the car all day."

"You'll perish in the heat," Flynn warned me. "You'll get bogged down in the melted asphalt and turn into a fossil like the saber-toothed tiger."

"I'm all sticky," Yvonne told us, "I'm going to take a shower."

"A bit of talcum is always walcum," Flynn said, mock delicate.

I put my boots back on, got my sunglasses and walked outside. There was a beer store a couple blocks back, easy in, easy out, drive through. I hoped they would sell it to me if I was on foot. The real errand was to be self-destructive and give Yvonne and Bobby Flynn a little time alone. Maybe something would happen that would finally make it blow between us, something I could point to. No more vibrations. Let's confront.

I walked through the heat haze along franchise row. Fish 'n' chips, roast-beef sandwiches, cheeseburgers, gasoline. The only one on foot on this four-lane highway, trudging along in the fumes, trying to locate the moment it all started going wrong. The night I left Yvonne's house to meet Flynn and find out Blowy was dead. But something was already wrong, otherwise I would never have left. It had to do with the case stalling. When all the evidence was in place, when Yvonne had stolen Mayo's paper and read it to me naked on the Legion's leather couch—and when nothing came of it. Blame Alden. Blame the world; it undoes love.

I bought two six-packs and went out into the wave of heat and car exhaust, walking faster on the way back. I opened the door to the motel room and heard the shower running. The bathroom door was open and behind it the shower curtain was half pushed back. Yvonne was naked with her hair wet and streaming. She looked free, she looked young again, she looked like the rose trellis. I took a step closer. Flynn was in there with her. His head and shoulders were bent and his eyes were closed. Yvonne had a good lather around his dick and she was jerking him off.

I put the beer on the air conditioner minus two cans for myself. I went outside, chose a metal lawn chair in front of our unit and sat back to watch another ruined sunset.

At nine-thirty we were in surveillance position around Mayo's rooming house on Emerson Street. We had to see him come out of there. I was not going to take action against the enemy and find out it was the wrong one. Yvonne was at the wheel of Angel at the corner, a half block from the house. I was in the forsythia directly under Mayo's window. Flynn, freshly jerked off and whatever else, was in the scrawny evergreens by the front door.

The street was alive with voices. People were out on their stoops. The darkness was not complete and our cover wasn't very good.

At twenty minutes to ten a car stopped in front of the rooming house. The driver honked the horn. A foot above my head I felt Mayo slam his window shut and I heard the counterweights swaying inside the wall. He had not latched the window shut.

The noise shifted to the front of the house. The door opening and closing. Then a car door being shut. The car pulling away fast from the curb.

Five minutes later Flynn and I met on the corner.

"What did you see, Swamp Fox?" he asked me.

"Nothing, Chicken Pox. It's what I heard. He didn't lock his window."

"Didn't or couldn't. I don't think this place comes with locks. Phew! I could smell the roach powder all the way from the front door."

"Did you see the enemy?"

"I didn't get a good view. The bushes were so low I had to stay flat on the ground until he passed. What can I tell you? He's the same size as Mayo. He walks like Mayo. But I couldn't get a real good look at him."

We walked toward Angel. Yvonne would not have gotten a better look than Flynn.

"I told you I have to see his face!"

"I'm sorry, Boo-Boo. I just didn't want to get seen."

We climbed into Angel. Yvonne went to slide over.

"Stay there," I told her. "You're driving us."

She started the engine.

"What would Blowy do?" I asked Flynn. "Or is this too trivial for the dead to get involved in?"

"Blowy agrees with you. You have to look into his face. But he must not see you."

"Great! What should I do? Be his mirror?"

"You can never get a straight answer from the dead," Flynn said sadly. "Now you know how it is."

For a minute I liked Flynn again. Or at least sympathized with him. "Let's go by the factory."

Flynn reached under the seat for the rest of the beer. It was warm by now. I leaned out the window and looked west, and saw the first flashes of heat lightning. Flat sheets of pink rose over the heavy, still treetops, lightning without thunder or storm. The earth was overcome by heat and trying to release whatever it could.

Yvonne drove us back to the plant. We bumped over the spur

line. She drove driving-school style, with her hands at ten and two o'clock, the way she learned to. Flynn sat between us, stiff and straight, drinking his warm beer.

"Let's stop at Mr. Bill's. I've got another plan."

We got the same booth. At the next table were two blacks who looked as though they worked across the street. I figured I had a better chance with them.

"Hey, can you tell me when's the next shift change?"

They looked up. They were having catfish. "Midnight."

"That's a different shift from the security guys?"

"Se-cur-i-ty!" They both laughed at the word. "Yeah, different shift. They couldn't have them changing shifts the same time we are."

"No?"

"They might forget to look in our satchels to see if we're stealing any tools!"

They both laughed again, as if the prospect were unthinkable.

"Do they really check you out?" I asked.

"They don't check shit! They just watch."

"We got a sort of a friend who works in security. We have a little bet to see whether we can get by him without him noticing us."

They nodded. "You've got to show your ID card."

"What's it look like?"

They took out their cards. We took some cards we had in our wallets to match size and color and position of the photo. Flynn still had his old Kensington school card, and wouldn't you know it? It fit best.

One of the guys leaned over to me. "You got a hat? Stick it in the front of your hat. Then just do a little nod when you walk by."

"You're not going in there?" Yvonne asked.

"Blowy said I had to see his face. No one has seen his face, right, Flynn? What if it's not him?"

Flynn shook his head. "There's not consensus on your plan."

"There is rarely consensus," I told him, "even within the same individual."

On their way out, the two black workers called, "See you on the graveyard shift!"

I WAS GLAD TO be alone at the wheel, the radio off, no sound but the flow of the hot prairie air through the windows, Flynn and Yvonne at the Dairyland Inn waiting for me and 5:00 AM in the way they saw fit. I stopped at a bar called the Vault in an old bank building, and found it full of students from the local liberal-arts college celebrating Earth Day. A girl dressed in overalls was wearing an engineer's cap and when she tired of it she hung it on the back of her chair. I got up and lifted it on my way out. A decent fit, though too new and clean. I popped open Angel's hood and got some grease from the top of her air cleaner. I parked the car a block from Mayo's guardhouse. I had my lunch bucket from Streets and Water, my brown uniform, my hat. I made four little notches on the front of it with my knife and stuck Flynn's old ID in it. A Kensington Krazy goes to work. I was ready for the graveyard shift.

I wanted to go in with a group but no one went to work that way at midnight. I hung back until a carpool came up, four men in their forties talking trailers and fishing holidays. I fell in behind them. I was counting on Mayo not having enough memory to recall who I was, or enough imagination to think we would ever return for him.

I went through the gate past the guardhouse window. The men in front of me had their IDs taped to their lunchboxes. They went through and I followed. I bent my head to show my card and the guard had to look up over my eye level. I had all the time in the world to see it was Tom Mayo in there. The heavy, square face, the lips a little open in anxious non-comprehension, the washed-out blue eyes. He looked like someone we could take out. I jerked my head straight and walked into the plant.

It turned out to be easier breaking in than breaking out. I had lost the men who went in ahead of me. I took the first turn down a hall that led away from Mayo's station and ended up in a corridor with locked offices along one side. This was no place for a worker who did the midnight shift. I took another hall and the floor began to move with a giant roaring. I followed the noise.

At the end of the hall was a set of insulated double doors. I opened them and it hit me: a noise so intense I wanted to scream. I jammed my fingers in my ears but it seemed to come through my mouth and eyes to attack my brain. I was on a catwalk and below were two enormous diesel engines in a pit, running full tilt, with men working on them wearing ear protectors. The noise was too strong to let me think. I saw a crane system, two steel rails and a metal roll-up door. I ran for it, along the catwalk, down a set of spiral stairs to the door. I hit the green Raise button, and when there was a foot showing between the bottom of the door and the cement floor I threw myself to the ground and rolled out into the calm, still air.

I was in the factory scrap yard. There were sheets of rusting steel stacked on skids. I followed a pair of rails to the fence; it was the spur line. The barbed wire on top of the fence was angled outward. I tossed my lunch box over and thirty seconds later I was on the other side with it.

YVONNE AND FLYNN were watching a black-and-white war movie on TV.

"We were just getting in the mood," Flynn said when I came in.

"Yeah? For what?"

He pointed to the rat-a-tat on the screen. "Make war, not love."

"Did you see him?" Yvonne remembered to ask.

"Yes."

"What's he like?"

I held out. "You'll see at six o'clock tomorrow."

Flynn stood up. "Now that you're back safely and we know that Mayo is who he is, I can sleep easy."

He grabbed the pillows off the bed.

"Sleep on that fold-up job," I told him.

"I wouldn't want to disturb you turtledoves. I'm going off to sleep in the bath." He slapped the pillows. "Just wake me up if you decide to take a shower."

I turned off the TV, the air conditioner and the lights. I stripped and got into bed. My ears were still hurting.

Yvonne got in beside me. I tried to remember the last time that happened. Then I put her hand on my dick.

"Do me like you did Flynn."

"You want that when you can have better?"

I tried to see her eyes in the light from the Arby's Roast Beef Sandwich sign.

"I was in the shower. I was washing my hair. When I opened my eyes there was Bobby, naked." She lowered her voice. "Behold Flynn the Loveless, he says. Love me. Then he starts coming at me. He had a hard-on. He got into the shower. I was afraid of . . . you know. So I gave him a release."

We listened to the tractor trailers go by toward the Interstate.

"His body is all old already. It gave me the creeps."

"But you did it anyway."

"Try being afraid of getting raped." She spat out the word. "You'll take the easy way out, I guarantee it."

We held each other for a while, tentatively, an awkward homecoming.

"I wonder what show Mr. Wrablik is watching."

"Don't torture us," she said.

Yvonne was loud when we finally made love, like she was forcing the pleasure out of her body. She protested, she pounded my shoulders. It was a kind of lamentation for everything we had been together.

I WAS AWAKE when the alarm went. When he heard me hit the button Flynn came out of the bathroom with a can of beer in his hand. He had not slept very well.

He popped the top.

"I kept this one in the sink, in cold water. But the water went warm overnight. Want some anyway?"

I took a sip. Yvonne stirred and and started to go back to sleep. Then she remembered where she was. She threw off the covers and I wanted to slap her across the face. She was naked, still wet and sweet-smelling from our lovemaking. Parading herself that way in front of Flynn. Maybe that was her idea of revenge. I didn't want to be used for it. I wanted her to keep our night together like something holy.

I looked at Flynn. He had turned his face away. I did too.

WE WERE OUT of the Dairyland Motel in ten minutes. The dawn was something hazy, gray and neglected in the eastern sky. I am used to dawn air being still and mat. But this dawn was not quiet. It was too dark to distinguish the clouds, but I could see gray masses churning in the sky and pushing downward to earth. The leaves turned in a wind that was jumpy and electric.

At deserted corners, the traffic lights changed futilely. Yvonne was at the wheel. I moved my gym bag up to the front seat. I unzipped it and touched everything we would need in the next thirty mintues. I felt anesthetized. The best way to go into this misadventure.

We waited for a light to change at the corner of Mayo's street. In the west, the darkest part of the sky, lightning flashed. It was not heat lightning; it carried real charge.

We stopped in front of Mayo's house at twenty-five minutes to six. Lights were burning on the top floor of the rooming house.

"What lives upstairs?" Flynn wondered.

"I don't know, but I hope it just fell asleep with the lights on."

"Scared of the dark," Yvonne put in.

I listened to Mayo's neighborhood through Angel's rolled-down window. The street was not having a good night. An air conditioner kicked in. Down the block, someone's drinking glass shattered in a sink and it felt so close I checked my cheek for splinters.

An electrical storm before dawn is something unnatural. No release of the day's heat, no glory in the skies. This dawn, the storm was turning sleepers in their beds and giving them seeds of a bad dream. The street lit up with a stroke of lightning and showed me Yvonne's and Flynn's faces, embalmed by lack of sleep. I waited for the roll of thunder; it did not come. The leaves rattled in the trees in a stronger gust of wind. Maliciously, the storm toyed with our nerves.

I zipped up my track bag and the noise made everyone jump.

"The picnic basket is ready," I told Flynn. "Are you ready for a picnic?"

"I guess I have to be."

We stepped out of the car into the moving, expectant air. I threw open my arms to get as much of it as I could after the stale air conditioning of the Dairyland. Above, the black clouds churned and reached down to us and moved eastward to obliterate the dawn.

For a moment in that wind I almost forgot Mayo, and this mission I had promised myself I would run. Then I heard the wheeze of Angel's parking brake as Yvonne let it off and the wet sound of the tires as she coasted her to the corner. We were on.

Flynn and I came around under Mayo's window. Flynn boosted me and I shinnied up the brick wall and got pretty good purchase on the window ledge. I tried sliding up the window but it would not go. I could feel the counterweights pulling down against me. I got out my knife and started cutting a notch into the wood. The sash was rotten, it hadn't been painted for years. I could have sliced my way right through it into Mayo's place.

There was another flash of lightning, more immediate this time. The treetops tossed and the wind on my bare arms made my hair stand up. In the next flash I saw my own reflection in Mayo's window, chalky and afraid.

"We're going to get seen," I heard Flynn murmur from below.

I chiseled a good enough hold on the frame to pry it up an inch or two. Then with one hand I reached down and got my fingers under the window. I was home free. I raised the window high and tumbled face first into Mayo's apartment.

I turned around, pulled Flynn in after me and closed the window. We waited in the silence for someone else to make the first move. Nothing stirred except for the survival scurry of the six-legged tenants. The place smelled like flat beer and roach powder. Early morning cocktail.

"Let's get comfortable," I told Flynn.

"Welcome to the land of the living dead."

We went to work. I got a butter knife from the rancid sink and unscrewed the plate over the light switch by the door. I ripped out a wire. Now we controlled the light. Then a flash of lightning illuminated the room and froze us in our tracks. I was sure every rooming-house insomniac in town could see us. Flynn crouched on the floor instinctively and I was going to make a joke about that but I didn't have time.

The thunderclap was so close it seemed to come from inside my head, worse than the testing pit at Mayo's factory. It tailed off and howling dogs replaced it.

"I wish it would just stop," Flynn complained from the floor.

"It's got to get itself over with first," I told him.

Flynn got up and did the room. He found a blackjack under Mayo's pillow.

"He's expecting visitors," Flynn said.

"I think it's to beat up the monsters in his bad dreams."

Water rocked through the pipes from upstairs and we both froze. It was a needless precaution. I opened the bag and got out the paraphernalia. A track starter's pistol.

"Where'd you get that?" Flynn said admiringly.

"You forget I was a teenage track star. I sort of accumulated it. It doesn't shoot, but at least it's cold."

Flynn handled it. "It's warm. Better put it in the fridge."

The inside of Mayo's fridge was a portrait of its renter. Jars of condiments, beer and salami turning green despite the nitrates. I let the fridge light shine on the rest of the room. On one wall were glossy posters of drag racers with flames shooting out the back. I half-expected to see a few copies of *Boy's Life* on the bedside table. Mayo was still a child.

I closed the fridge door.

"This is a kid's apartment," I said. "It's sick."

"It stinks," Flynn agreed.

"But it still stinks a lot less than where Chuck Alden is at."

Flynn cocked his head like he hadn't heard right. "I'd forgotten all about Chuck Alden, do you know that? I don't really care any more where Alden is."

"All right, Flynn, I won't bring him up any more. It was one of those leftover impulses from back when we cared about that kind of stuff."

I had a quick, righteous flash: pick up the gym bag and all the goddamned paraphernalia and walk out into the storm. Leave the dead in peace, each in his appointed hell.

Then out on the street a car door slammed. Male voices loud and sloppy hollering out there.

"We'll have to finish this discussion at a later date," Flynn said.

"Yeah, later. Never. Now it's time for the real storm."

I got the pistol out of the fridge. It had barely had time to cool down. Flynn unzipped the bag and spread out everything we would need. Mayo was fencing with the lock housing on the other side of the door, tap, tap, tap with his key until he finally got it in. Then the door swung open and he walked right in front of us.

He hit the light switch.

"This fucking hole!" he swore at the darkness.

He dropped what he was holding, a plastic six-pack strap with one beer attached. He moved clumsily across the room with one hand stretched out. He wanted the kitchen light fast. Maybe he was afraid of the dark.

"Trouble time!" Flynn announced very loudly.

Mayo wheeled toward the voice in the dark to hit it. I came in from behind and pulled up his shirt and stuck the pistol against his skin. The violence thing was automatic. I knew exactly what to do. Like everyone else, I'd rehearsed it plenty of times in movie houses and in front of the TV set.

"Just stop right there!" I spoke into Mayo's ear. "Keep calm and I won't shoot."

"Take it easy. You wouldn't want to turn your average stereo rip-off into a murder, would you?"

"I don't have a stereo," Mayo protested.

"But we don't know that. We'll have to take a look around."

Flynn came in with the blindfold, one of those elasticized things that keep your ears warm in winter. He clapped it around Mayo's eyes before the lightning could show him who we were.

"Now put your hands down to your sides, nice and easy, or I'll shoot," I told him. "I won't kill you, I'll just sever your spinal cord and you'll spend the rest of your life in a wheelchair spoiling your shorts."

Mayo obeyed and Flynn got the handcuffs off the top of the bag and snapped them on him.

"Sorry to have to do this." Flynn did his jaunty burglar bit. "Here, let me get you some beer. I see you've got one left."

He poured a little into a dirty glass from Mayo's sink.

"We're refined stereo rip-off artists," he told him, "we serve beer in a glass."

Flynn got the vial from the bag and shook the tab of acid into the beer. I had had to deal with Mafia types to get it. The new dream merchants. A giant hit, enough for a couple experienced freaks and cruelly laced with speed to keep the hallucinations nervous and stomach-sick. Kensington Krazy pharmaceuticals.

An old freak proverb says that if you have a bad trip you don't see anything that was not already inside your mind. That's what we were counting on for Mayo.

Flynn tilted the glass back. Mayo opened his lips. I could hear his throat working, swallowing the poison.

"I'm going to have some too, if you don't mind." For a moment I feared the worst, but Flynn took a pull from the can. "This is thirsty work."

He poured the rest of the can into Mayo's glass, thoroughly enjoying the power trip. "That's all you get. I can't have you getting too high on me now."

"I know you from somewhere. Where do I know you from?"

When Mayo finally spoke it was a shock. His voice had lost its smirk, he'd gotten passive. Of course, there was a gun in his back, that might have helped.

"Sure, you know us. You knew us when we were for peace and love. We've changed since."

Then I motioned to Flynn to put in the gag. From the way he danced around in front of him I could tell he was still afraid of Mayo, even handcuffed and on his way up on acid. Finally he got around to popping the gag in Mayo's mouth, which put an end to the conversation.

Flynn clipped a dog leash to Mayo's cuffs. I poked the barrel of the starter's pistol into his kidneys.

"Let's go for a walk," I told him.

Mayo tried to say something but he forgot he had the gag in. It came out all muffled. Maybe he was wondering about the stereo.

Flynn kept the leash tight and I stayed behind with the gun. We went down the hallway in formation. At the end of the hall the door was left open to get some cool air into this tenement, and beyond it the street, suddenly illuminated with strobes of reddish-white light, like blood, I thought, like the illumination rounds of wartime. When the thunder cracked Mayo gave a little start, as if he was going to run, and I felt Flynn pull hard to rein him in. The wind threw the door back on its hinges with a bang and the rain came marching down Mayo's street in curtains. Everything unreal in the strobes of light: trees bent at impossible angles, the crack of falling limbs, that roar in the sky of the storm train, whole sections of the block visible as if it were day, but in a mat, dead, chalky light, and through it Yvonne rolling Angel toward us, the engine inaudible in the storm's roar, but the car appearing in lightning flashes along the street. I pushed Mayo off with the starter's pistol and we ran into the slanting rain, Flynn pulling the leash hard. Yvonne swung the back door open for us, we pushed Mayo onto the floor and got on top of him. As Yvonne was pulling away from the curb I got the door shut. I did not know if anyone had seen us, or what their eyes told them if they had.

The landscape swam by. Mayo jumped at every crack of thunder and Flynn and I tried to make ourselves heavy on his back. In five minutes it was all over. I heard the windshield wipers stop and the road go dry under our tires. The sun was coming up again in the washed eastern sky.

"Happy Independence Day," I wished everyone.

Yvonne put us onto the I-90 headed for Kensington. The district would still be slumbering on this Sunday morning, when we would witness against Tom Mayo. Whatever that would prove to be.

I HAD DONE a little acid and had not liked it. No one had to drag me to the nearest hip doctor to get pumped full of Thorazine; I just did not enjoy being out of control. When I wanted to think a thought, I could picture only the electrochemical structure of the thought in my brain, synapses being leaped, a crisscross of yellow and blue wires, lights glowing like the board of a pinball machine. The thought got lost; I was helpless. Then there was the intensification, the self-consciousness about every part of the body. The tongue lying like an inert, soft animal in the mouth, the scrotum hanging comical and uncomfortable between the legs, rubbing and banging and sending out mixed pain and pleasure signals. Mayo was supposed to experience all that and more, whipped on by a seasoning of speed like ground glass in a salad. He was supposed to see himself. That was part of our witnessing. That was supposed to be righteous.

We had not administered acid to give him revelation. I did not want him touching God's starry robe. Acid was a cruel practical joke with unknown consequences. But I was skeptical about acid's revelations, despite what the cautionary freak proverb said. What was Mayo supposed to see? Blood running down the walls of his mind like a cheap horror movie? Chuck Alden popping out of his shallow grave like a jack-in-the-box?

Mayo was getting twitchy with speed on the floor of the backseat. In his position of sensory deprivation, it could not have been too pleasant. Blindfolded and handcuffed and bent in two. But whatever was happening inside his mind, he was still capable of forming intention: he spat out the gag.

"You fuckers," he said.

So banal it was startling.

"He can't be up if he's talking like that," I assessed.

"I'm not going to be insulted by an animal like that," Yvonne said from the front. "Get him to shut up."

She did not like the situation: a speeding car with a pathological mass of muscle meat in the back.

"He can't shut up until he's stated his case," I explained to her.

"What are you going to do with him?" she asked, sounding proprietary toward the prisoner.

"He's going to stand trial."

"He's going to talk to the judge!" Flynn said happily. "To Blowy Bloedell, People's Judge. For as I sat here, anxious yet needing a coffee, Blowy visited me to say he wishes to be judge."

"I thought it wasn't cool to judge," I reminded Flynn.

"That's okay. This is an imaginary judge."

"In that case I've got just the courtroom."

I fished a key from my pocket and dangled it.

"This is the key to the Hole. To the gate of the Hole. Which I pilfered and copied the last time I made a delivery for Streets and Water—for the forgetfulness squad, as Yvonne calls it."

"You guys are getting crazy again! Who's tripping here, him or you?" Yvonne cried.

In the backseat, Flynn and I looked at each other. We let the question pass.

I had a go at Mayo instead. "You're going on trial," I told him. "A trial before an imaginary judge. What do you think about that?"

He did not tell us. His teeth were clenched and his mouth shut tight like he was having an attack of lockjaw. He must have caught some gum or tongue because a little blood drooled out of one corner of his mouth.

"I guess by now you've figured out we don't care about your stereo. We're Kensington folks, just like you. And you know who we dug up for this special occasion? Chuck Alden himself! Remember, ducks and bunnies? Remember how you used to want drugs, body drugs? Well, we got you some. Remember Chuck Alden? He's going to be part of the trial too. Maybe you'll even get to shake hands with him!"

"The judge," Mayo said through clenched teeth, trying to keep control. "The judge is fucking my mother. That's how I got out."

"His lawyer was fucking his mother," Flynn corrected him, "that's what my leaky lawyer said."

"You can't correct someone on acid," I told Flynn. "Maybe he's right, maybe it was the judge too. Anything's possible in Cook County."

"*My* judge is above such fleshly interference."

"More power to him."

"That's why they sent me away, so he could fuck her better that way. I'm not in the next room any more when he fucks his whore. Then he jingles his change. Mama, don't fuck that man any more."

"Disgusting," said Yvonne.

"Is this what criminals have come to?" Flynn asked no one in particular.

"I wanted to be a man, but they sent me away, that was their plan. The lawyer got me free, then he said I'm not innocent, I'm guilty! On the day he came back from the court, he told me I'm guilty, I'll have to go away to stay."

"Mayo, any man will defend your innocence if he gets paid enough."

"Are you guilty?" Yvonne demanded from the front seat.

The walls of Mayo's ego were still a little too sturdy. He would not submit to the question.

"Of course you're guilty!" she screamed at him.

"Patience, patience," I told her, "the trial hasn't even begun yet."

WE REACHED KENSINGTON before the first lawn mower revved into action, long before the first church bell beckoned. The solid citizens were still solid blocks in their beds. Yvonne exited the Stevenson Expressway and drove to the Gilbert Avenue site. My key got us inside the ex-Hole in no time. It was like we ran the place.

A little mist hung over the low spots in the dump. It was real bucolic. We all got out of Angel.

"The courtroom is over there, by the underground stream," I instructed. "And watch your step, innocent and guilty alike, the last thing you want here is a cut."

Flynn played out the dog leash and Mayo loped across the garbage fields like a freak being led to the sideshow. He was bent into a defensive hunch. Like someone on a trip who does not want to be there, protecting the little bit of ego stability he has left.

We climbed hill and dale with Mayo following blindly along until we reached the edge of the sinkhole. I looked down the steep slope and saw the dilemma: no matter what you poured down it, the hole never filled up.

"On the shores of this underground river, I declare this trial come to order!"

I pulled the elastic band from Mayo's eyes. He stared. He tried to assimilate.

"Do you recognize this place, Tom?"

He stared.

"You should. It's the Hole! And you're the reason it doesn't look like the Hole any more."

"You're anticipating the charges," Flynn cut me off. "The dignity of the court demands a minimum of furnishing. I see some doorless fridges that might be used."

"They shouldn't be here. This is a clean landfill."

Flynn gave me a hateful look. How dare I introduce an uncalled-for incursion of reality into the masquerade?

He dragged an old icebox-type refrigerator to the edge of the sinkhole.

"The witness stand," Flynn deemed, and he made Mayo sit down in the empty cavity where the door should have been.

"The judge's gavel." He picked up something that could have been a tie-rod.

"And a bench for the combination prosecution and jury." He banged at the side of a staved-in freezer chest.

We sat down facing Mayo. He looked uncomfortable with his ass stuck in an empty icebox and his hands pinned behind his back.

"Why don't you take off his handcuffs?" I said to Flynn. "You can't try someone in chains, it's not the American way. He's not going anywhere."

Flynn unlocked the handcuffs and threw them down the sink-hole. They hit the bottom with a wet thud.

"Chains in the void," he declared.

"You've got a gavel, Flynn. Do you have a judge to go with it?"

"Yes, of course... Will the judge please emerge from his chambers?"

We all waited. I looked up at the hazy sky. It did not open, Blowy did not appear like at Lourdes, all dripping with shrapnel wounds, to take the tie-rod from Flynn's hands and be seated at a derelict fridge.

There was a long moment of silence. It seemed to go on forever, like at a Quaker meeting.

"I believe the judge is among us," Flynn announced.

Mayo's eyes darted left and right. There was a look of hostile submission on his face.

"The judge pulled down his pants. My mother said will you please go into your room, I must discuss with this gentleman if you want to be free. Well, I don't want to be free!"

"Your mother is a call girl and you're the son of a call girl and, what's worse, a mama's boy. And the judge we've got here is invisible. His flesh is dead so he's not interested in your mother. And the fact that he's dead is being blamed on you in certain quarters, making you an escaped goat in the first degree. So he'll probably do something about your desire not to be free."

"Will you read out the charges," Flynn said, "so we can get this trial underway?"

"The charges? There are charges?"

"Come on, you guys!" Yvonne complained, "stop word tripping!"

Flynn and I laughed. Telling us to stop word tripping under the circumstances was like telling people in a tavern to stop drinking. What else were we to do in a garbage dump at seven-thirty on a Sunday morning on Independence Day weekend? Perform acts of natural justice?

"All right, I'll read the charges."

"Read them in a way that a guy with a dissolving ego can understand," Flynn put in.

"This business about acid dissolving ego borders is strictly a poetic concept," I told him. "Now, I'm about to read the charges without word tripping."

"Good luck."

I looked around and counted the little crimes and discontents among us. I started there.

"The guilty party known as Mayo to us but, to himself, unknown at this time, is charged with causing the destruction of this once-marvelous playpen where now we stand. He is charged with contributing to the works of garbage contractors and colonial-style house builders. He is charged with poisoning a beautiful relationship between Yvonne Chezevski, only daughter and only child of Sgt.-Det. Chezevski, and the prosecutor—that's me. This aforesaid poisoning is part of the greater war of the sexes fought around the concept of separate but equal orgasms. In other words, Mayo, you are charged with killing the 1960s, such as we imagined them to be. Do you understand the charges?"

"Before asking that question," Flynn said, "Blowy would like to add his death to the charges, as a result of indirect circuits that I don't need to describe. And out of solidarity with the dead, he would ask you not to forget the murder of Chuck Alden, especially on this holy ground."

"You have a point, Flynn."

"I want to add something too," Yvonne said. "The rape of Janie James."

Her charge left a hole in the morning. We had long since forgotten that abdication.

"Be it so entered. Mayo, do you understand the charges? Do you have any reply?"

He rocked. He hummed. He chewed his gums so hard blood ran from the corners of his mouth again. All our beautiful words washed over him with no effect.

"Disgusting," Yvonne complained.

"Massive ego loss," Flynn diagnosed. "And to think that was some people's objective."

"Maybe he's just going with the flow."

"I shudder to think."

"*He* can't go with the flow," Yvonne insisted.

"It could be worse," I told her, "he could have achieved Zen illumination right here in the garbage dump. That would have been a bummer."

"I say massive ego loss," Flynn said as Mayo went on rocking and humming.

"Massive ego loss, my ass! He's in total control. Either that or he doesn't have the imagination to bad-trip. It's just not working."

"He's not *listening* to us." Yvonne was close to tears.

We had been good commandos, we had captured and immobilized a large and dangerous quantity of muscle meat. But now we could get inside it. Or maybe we had gotten too far in, where an incident, a smudge like Chuck Alden meant nothing.

Flynn got up from the fridge.

"You're a novice in psychosis," he told me. "Lean back on your Frigidaire and watch as I bad-trip the accused out of his brains. Vengeance is within reach."

Flynn licked his psychic chops. Then he moved in real close on Mayo, still bent inside his icebox witness stand. Flynn reached down and scooped up a handful of semi-clean fill. He held it in front of Mayo's face.

"Look at this stuff, it's alive. It's like a cemetery, it's made out of dead stuff that's started living again under the ground."

He made Mayo sniff it. I knew what it smelled like: chalk dust and broken stones, not the graveyard.

"Somewhere around here you wasted Alden. I wonder if there aren't a few pieces of his bone and guts in this little handful."

It was the classic bad-trip question. Scary monsters. Blood and slime oozing down the walls like an old horror movie. Old-hat stuff based on cause and effect and guilt and things that were not working any more.

"I wonder what kind of sound it made?" Flynn had his face in Mayo's face. "You know, when the rock hit his head? Did it make a plop? Did he scream or didn't he have time to? Did his head crack open like an egg? Did you get to see what was inside?"

Mayo was not responding to treatment. Flynn's number was making a bigger impression on Yvonne and me. But then again, we were rational.

"I heard Alden was still alive when you buried him in that grave you dug. At least he was still breathing, he could have been saved. But he started breathing in dirt and he was too wasted to push it away from his face. First it got in his nose and then it stopped up his lungs and finally it killed him. Picture it, Mayo, all that dirt stuck up your nose and pressing around your face."

Flynn threw his handful of dirt on Mayo's chest. Mayo let it lie there.

"You want to get free but you can't. You're too wasted. Your arms just won't work any more. The dirt keeps pressing down harder and harder because someone's throwing it on top of your grave. You want to yell, Hey, don't do that, I'm down here, I'm still alive, but when you open your mouth a whole shitload of dirt gets in and besides, you realize that's just what they want to do up there on the earth: bury you. And the dirt tastes really bad, you want to clamp your mouth shut hard but there's a rock in there and you can't do it. Ever try to swallow a stone? The dirt is starting to keep the air from getting in. You want to stop breathing because you're breathing dirt but you can't because breathing isn't under your control. You want to fight it and keep the dirt out of your body where it will kill you but you don't have the strength to—can you feel that, Mayo?"

But Mayo did not feel it. He rocked and chewed on his tongue and the insides of his cheeks. He talked to himself. He was working out a private matter.

"That's enough, Grand Inquisitor," I told Flynn. "You're only spooking yourself. You want him to fly into some kind of textbook bad trip—that's so conventional!"

"All right," Flynn shot back. "Screw him. He's yours if you think you know what to do with him."

"This is a dump," I told Flynn. "Why don't we just dump him?"

"We can't just leave him here," Yvonne wailed. She was witnessing natural justice being denied, and with it her last chance to help her father. "Fuck you guys! He screwed us up then. He's screwing us up now too! Can't we *do* anything about it?"

"You've got the judge," I taunted Flynn, "that's the main equipment. Make your playmate do something."

Then it was Mayo's turn to join the madness.

"The judge sent me away," he told his story plaintively. "And

I don't understand why. I'm innocent, so why can't I stay? Innocent people can stay, but no, I have to go away, so my mother won't have to say, later, when Tommy goes away. But one day Tommy's going to come back to play.''

But Mayo wasn't giving us madness. He wasn't word tripping. This time I listened to him, and a sick thrill came over me. Acid *was* revealing—and what calm and purposeful revelations these were. He was giving us the cue. He was onto something much deeper than Chuck Alden. For him, Alden was no more than a smudge on his consciousness. Fuck Flynn's pretend judge. A new judge was emerging, I could tell by the whisper of the wing of the Angel of Death over my shoulder this Kensington Sunday morning.

Justice was in reach. I grabbed the pretend judge's gavel out of Flynn's hands and presented it to Mayo. It was a mean-looking automobile tie-rod.

"Here's the toy that makes a boy a man," I urged Mayo. "If you had your way, where would you play? What would you say to the man that put you in the can? How would you make that man pay? What would you do if he took your mama away?"

I placed the tie-rod in Mayo's hands. He cradled it like a baby. We were about to do a righteous thing.

Mayo and I understood each other. "Tommy's gone away," he told me, "but he ain't gone to stay."

"Cause one day there'll be hell to pay when he comes home to play."

I motioned to Yvonne.

"Give me the keys. I've got us a destination. That's more than what we have now."

Mayo and I went walking toward Angel. Yvonne and Flynn lagged behind.

"What about Blowy? What about the judge?" Flynn wanted to know.

"This young man," I nodded at Mayo, "doesn't need a judge, at least not a dead one. He's got one inside, courtesy of the wonder drug. He watched us play and now he wants to play too. Judge and jury."

I spoke gentle rhyme into Tom Mayo's ear all the way to the car. I'd never seen a man treat rusted iron with such gentle respect. He was right to: it was his tool of deliverance. And ours too.

Harold Bartlesby and Judge Gallagher had freed him in the world's eyes. Now he was going to free himself.

I sat Mayo in the front seat. Yvonne and Flynn did not go for it. You never put dangerous cargo in the front seat where it can fool with the controls. But I knew Mayo. He wanted to go where I wanted to take him.

Just in case, I tested him. I drove through the gate, out of the Hole, and stopped. I got out to lock the gate behind us and left the car running and the key in the ignition. Mayo waited docilely for his driver to return.

On the way over I comforted him with nonsense rhyme.

"You made Chuck Alden pay, but Chuck Alden ain't hay, not in the game you're going to play. Are you man enough to have it your own way?"

"I'm no good," he confided in me, staring out the windshield. "If I was any good, my father wouldn't have fucked my mother and my mother wouldn't have fucked a dog."

For a moment I tried to follow Mayo's logic and wonder who that dog was. Wisely, I did not pursue the connections. I felt in a state of unnatural, calm attention; contours and colors were sharper. The feeling was my own clarity of decision. We were in the better part of Kensington now. I heard the swishing of a sprinkler starting, and a lawn-mower engine. At the end of the street, where the neighborhood changed, the California Zephyr flew by the level crossing.

I spared a thought for old Mr. Clouds and my brief clarity was shattered. Station Wagon of Fools. I pictured the four of us trapped inside Angel, driving on forever, the gas needle by some malevolent miracle never dropping, driving the Kensington streets unable to stop, not even at a doughnut shop for coffee, because Tom Mayo and his trip were an embarrassment to us. He was the sixth finger the ashamed hand must hide. He was our bad-vibes reflection. We could not stop at the Jack-in-the-Box because the waitress would recognize us and ask, "What are you doing with him? Are you this corrupted?" And we would have to answer, "Yes, we've gone with the times."

My easy-trauma knee was sending me pain messages: *Get off this trip. Bail out.* I crossed the tracks and turned onto Ashland Avenue. The land of ashes.

"Where are we going?" Yvonne's voice was plaintive and defeated from the backseat.

I felt a quick flash of pain for what we had been, and knew my time of mourning was just beginning.

I turned around and faced her. "We're releasing him into captivity."

"But I wanted justice!"

"Justice will be yours. Though I can't guarantee how useful it will be to you personally. But I bet the Sgt.-Det. would approve."

I stopped Angel behind a massive, cream-colored Cadillac in front of Lynda Mayo's apartment block. Harold Bartlesby's car. Mayo looked at me expectantly. He was still cradling the rusty tie-rod.

"There's your house," I told him. "They're inside."

Mayo assimilated the information. He didn't need rhyme from me any more. He considered the low, square apartment block in the empty Kensington morning. People sleeping inside. Not yet awoken to their son's return.

"You be the judge," I said to Mayo.

"Tom will go away, so we'll have a chance to play. But when Tom has his way, there'll be hell to pay."

Then he got out. He was really going to do it.

Yvonne understood. "He's going to kill her!" she screamed from the back. "Stop him!"

Mayo opened the door to the block and stepped inside. He wasn't cradling his judge's gavel anymore. He was gripping it real tight.

Everything that goes down comes around.

I pulled out onto Ashland Avenue from behind the lawyer's long car. I was giving the Sgt.-Det. satisfaction, even if I was losing his daughter. But what the hell, in a way I felt for him the most. I stopped Angel at the next corner and left her motor idling, then swung open the door and put my foot on the pavement.

I walked into a morning of Kensington church bells tolling above their deserted sanctuaries.